# CATS DON'T NEED COFFINS

**DOLORES HITCHENS**

Writing as
D.B. Olsen

*Introduction by*
**OTTO PENZLER**

**AMERICAN MYSTERY CLASSICS**

*Penzler Publishers*
*New York*

This is a work of fiction. Names, characters, places, and incidents either are the product of the author's imagination or are used fictitiously. Any resemblance to actual persons, living or dead, businesses, companies, events, or locales is entirely coincidental.

Published in 2026 by Penzler Publishers
58 Warren Street, New York, NY 10007
penzlerpublishers.com

Distributed by Simon & Schuster



Cover image: Andy Ross
Cover design: Mauricio Diaz

Paperback ISBN 978-1-61316-746-5
Hardcover ISBN 978-1-61316-745-8

Library of Congress Control Number: 2025942661

Printed in the United States of America

9 8 7 6 5 4 3 2 1

OTTO PENZLER PRESENTS
AMERICAN MYSTERY CLASSICS

# CATS DON'T NEED COFFINS

**Dolores Hitchens** (1907–1973) was a highly prolific mystery author who wrote under multiple pseudonyms and in a range of styles. A large number of her books were published under the D. B. Olsen moniker (under which her "Cat" series was originally published), but she is perhaps best remembered today for her later novel, *Fool's Gold*, published under her own name, which was adapted as *Band a part* by Jean-Luc Godard.

**Otto Penzler,** the creator of American Mystery Classics, is also the founder of the Mysterious Press (1975); MysteriousPress.com (2011), an electronic-book publishing company; and New York City's Mysterious Bookshop (1979). He has won a Raven, the Ellery Queen Award, two Edgars (for the *Encyclopedia of Mystery and Detection*, 1977, and *The Lineup*, 2010), and lifetime achievement awards from NoirCon and *The Strand Magazine*. He has edited more than 80 anthologies and written extensively about mystery fiction.

# INTRODUCTION

THE SERIES of thirteen books by Dolores Hitchens under the pseudonym D.B. Olsen isn't exactly what most readers would expect when they pick up a book about a little old lady and her cat.

They may sound like cozies but they aren't, not really. All the accoutrements of a saccharine soft-boiled detective story exist: a home with faded Victorian furniture, a seventy-year-old spinster who smells of lavender, known always as Miss Rachel, and a sister, Miss Jennifer, who won't allow liquor in the house and tirelessly works on her embroidery. When excited, both ladies are likely to use such explosive terms as "fiddle-faddle." And, of course, a cat, this one named Samantha. In an early book, *Alarm of the Black Cat* (1942), she was, strangely, described as marmalade but in this one is "black as a midnight sky."

In *Cats Don't Need Coffins* (1946), they are summoned to Miriam Hamilton's house for the ostensible purpose of collecting an inheritance. It seems that Miriam's father cheated Miss Rachel's father years ago and she wants to make reparations as a moral duty. Miss Rachel is skeptical because she doesn't believe anyone could have swindled her very shrewd father but is too curious about the surprising opportunity and prepares to make the visit.

As in many of the adventures of the prim old ladies, Miss Jennifer refuses to accompany her but, inevitably, changes her mind and off they go, accompanied by Samantha.

Miss Rachel, older by two years, is brave and curious, willing (well, in fact, eager) to participate in any adventure that presents itself. Her sister, on the other hand, is timid and seemingly fragile but allows herself to be bullied (let's say persuaded) by Miss Rachel, though it is fair to wonder if, deep down, she is almost as ready to get involved in events that she eventually finds interesting. Despite her frequent objections to doing pretty much anything, she winds up doing them anyway, often with low-key gusto.

When they arrive at the massive mansion, Miriam is nowhere to be seen and Misses Rachel and Jennifer feel an eerie tension among the guests and household. Not only have none of them been properly greeted, they seem to be eyeing each other suspiciously.

The first sight of the missing hostess occurs when a nervous maid takes Miss Rachel to Miriam's bedroom, telling her that she "seems very queer. I'm afraid there's something wrong. Will you come and take a look and see what should be done?" Something is indeed wrong but nothing can be done. Miriam is in her bed, murdered so brutally that her bones have been broken. (As mentioned previously, Dolores Hitchens' books are emphatically not cozy.)

A long steel knitting needle, a diabolical-looking doll, and oddly behaving members of the household combine to introduce numerous surprises, inexplicable events, and questions for Miss Rachel to explain while the local sheriff does what he can to ignore her suggestions.

The series of Rachel Murdock mysteries by Julia Clara

Catherine Maria Dolores Robins Norton Birk Olsen Hitchens (1907-1973), better known to mystery readers as Dolores Hitchens, was published under the nom de plume D.B. Olsen, as was another series, featuring Professor Pennyfeather. Friends who find themselves in trouble frequently ask Pennyfeather for help because his classical education is invaluable in organizing his thoughts, leading to reasoned solutions to complex problems.

Hitchens also wrote numerous novels under own name, as well as five in collaboration with her last husband, Hubert A. (Bert) Hitchens, who had been a railway detective. She had previously been married to Beverley S. Olsen, a radio operator on a merchant vessel, and soon after, in 1938, began to write as D(olores) B(everley) Olsen.

After her marriage to Bert, they collaborated on a series of railroad mysteries from 1957 to 1964.

The prolific Dolores also wrote many highly regarded standalone mysteries, including *Fool's Gold* (1958), which was published in the prestigious Library of America volume *Women Crime Writers of the 1950s: Four Suspense Novels* (2015), along with Charlotte Armstrong (*Mischief*), Patricia Highsmith (*The Blunderer*), and Margaret Millar (*The Beast in View*). It was later published separately as a paperback by Library of America.

Hitchens also wrote two mysteries as Dolan Birkley (*Blue Geranium*, 1944) and (*The Unloved*, 1965) and one as Noel Burke (*Shivering Bough*, 1942).

*Fool's Gold* was filmed by Jean-Luc Godard in 1964 with the title *Band of Outsiders*. It is the tragic story of two teenage boys recently released from a juvenile detention center and an orphaned girl who make the decision to commit what looks like a simple robbery only to see it become so complicated that it whirls out of their control.

With the publication of this novel and others, such as *Sleep with Strangers* (1956) and *Sleep with Slander* (1961), Hitchens showed a wide range of tone and subjects, from the (relatively) benign traditional detective story to a tough, more realistic, almost hard-boiled style.

In *Cats Don't Need Coffins*, the tone may be gentle but there is no escaping the author's intention to show that Miss Rachel is as tough as Philip Marlowe, even if she has white hair and wears taffeta over her thin body.

—Otto Penzler
May 2025

# CHAPTER ONE

Miss Jennifer Murdock, a plain, spinsterish little old lady of seventy-two, put on the most disapproving expression she knew and looked across the hump of her embroidery hoop at her sister.

Miss Rachel, a Dresden-china model with white silky curls and a ruffled pink dimity morning dress, smiled back sweetly. Miss Rachel never could tell in advance which of her smiles might have effect: the mollifying simper or the faintly wistful twitch of the lips or the intelligent grin. As a rule Jennifer didn't like any of them.

Jennifer didn't like the one she used now.

"There are acts, Rachel, which no real lady will stoop to." Miss Jennifer stabbed the material in the hoop and began to wind a french knot. "One of them is to open other people's mail. I hate to bring up anything reflecting on Mother's people—you always defend them so—but you might just remember Uncle Theodore for a minute."

Miss Rachel looked at the letter in her hand and the letter opener lying on the little rosewood table before her. "It isn't actually mail, Jennifer," she defended. "It's just a letter. A note. Mail has to be put in a postbox before it's legal. And anyway, if there's money in the letter I'll put it all back. Not like Uncle Theodore, poor man."

"Don't defend a criminal, Rachel."

"Mother always said that his Romeo was magnificent."

"It didn't entitle him to Mr. Lettish's check. Now, Rachel, since Miriam has trusted you——"

"Miriam never trusted anyone farther than she could watch them. You know it just as well as I do. And if she wanted Mr. What's-his-name——" She turned the letter over to study the writing on its front surface, the elegant and forceful penmanship which reminded her so well of Miriam, and of how Miriam could look as though she were a queen enduring the company of peddlers. "If she wanted Mr. Dewel to get this letter without my peeking into it first she shouldn't have put in something that rattles."

"He'll know, Rachel. He'll know you opened it and he'll perhaps tell Miriam and then . . . Miriam can be so forthright in what she says." Miss Jennifer shivered as though some of Miriam's forthrightness had recurred to her.

"There is a word for Miriam but I am not going to pain you by speaking it," said Miss Rachel. "And the way to describe her manner of speech is not forthright. It's rude. Now I think that if I just slip the knife through this side opening . . . like this . . . and work the paper a bit back and forth . . ."

Miss Jennifer folded her embroidery into a packet. "I won't stay and see you break every rule of civilized conduct. At the age of seventy, taking up the robbery of mail—and——"

Miss Rachel had gotten the side flap open and had put an eye to it. "This is the queerest thing that ever happened to me," she murmured. Then she poured three small black flat objects from the envelope into her palm.

Miss Jennifer didn't go away. She bent closer to look; which was what Miss Rachel had known she would do, all along.

This ravishment of Miriam Hamilton's letter to Mr. Joe Dewel always marked afterward, for Miss Rachel, the beginning of the affair she chose to call the Case of the Dismal Doll.

Though the broken and frightful doll didn't appear until afterward, in the black night outside Miriam's window, there was, even in the beginning, at the time of Miss Rachel's opening of the letter, a sense of gentle and beautiful things bent to ugly purposes, a twisted incongruity as though the odor of blackdamp had risen suddenly from a cluster of violets.

For the three black objects which rattled forth from the letter were wisteria seeds.

Miss Jennifer, the conscientious gardener, had known that at once.

What she hadn't known—and mercifully for Miss Jennifer—was that a flowery hideousness was beginning even then to unfold, that the wisteria seeds were to gather to them other objects used for purposes no one had foreseen: the little fuchsias whose dying was part of an ugly revenge; the lantana which covered an eavesdropper; the small night-blooming light that shone on bloody terror; the tractor which plowed no field but Death's.

Miss Jennifer, conscious then of only a mild curiosity, looked at her sister Rachel. "Well, you know now. They're just seeds."

"Awfully big ones, aren't they?" queried Miss Rachel, used to the star dust off petunias and poppies.

"Wisteria. Father's nurseryman showed me some, long ago. I stole one because it looked like licorice. It didn't taste that way." She sighed.

Miss Rachel was peering again into the letter. "There's a note too. Just one line. It's Miriam's writing."

"No, Rachel, that's spying!"

"There has to be a reason for Miriam sending Mr. Dewel wisteria seeds. Especially in such a roundabout way. Why didn't she simply mail them to him?" She drew out a slip of paper gently.

The note was quite brief.

*Now you feel better, don't you?*

M.H.

Miss Jennifer murmured the message to herself, then grew gradually crimson. "She *knew* you'd be into it! Oh, Rachel, she's making fun! How could you have fallen into the trap she set with this silly letter?"

But Miss Rachel was frowning at the note, her face thoughtful and withdrawn. "No, Jennifer. Miriam never used such restraint in her life toward anyone who might open her mail. If she had thought I'd read this, and the note was a joke on me, I'm sure the language would be much stronger. Sulphuric, in fact." She spent a long moment in silence while Jennifer made clucking noises of disagreement. "This message, and the seeds, are for Mr. Dewel," Miss Rachel decided. "I wonder what on earth they mean? Well, we'll see how he acts when he receives them."

Mr. Dewel rang their doorbell at eight o'clock that evening, just as they had settled themselves in the living room after dinner. Miss Jennifer was unraveling some of the mistakes in embroidery which the day's nervous upsets had caused her to make. She was afraid that Mr. Dewel wouldn't be fooled by Rachel's paste job on the letter. As for Miss Rachel, she was watchful but serene.

Mr. Dewel gave a first impression of being plump and reddish. Then he came into the bright light of the living room and

Miss Rachel saw that the plumpness was overlaid with a haggard look, as though a wax Santa Claus were beginning to melt around the edges, and that the reddish blush was probably liquor. He was somewhat over forty, going bald, clean but mended as to linen, and not much taller than Miss Rachel herself. He had light brown eyes with a sad, doggy expression. As he bowed to the two little old ladies the gray serge rumpled across his plumpness and his chins wobbled. When he talked there was a loud smell of gum and breath perfume and whisky.

Mr. Dewel accepted their invitation to sit down. He asked uncertainly if Miriam had written about him and whether she had explained his errand.

"She said you were calling on business," said Miss Jennifer. "She didn't say what business. I'm wary of having any dealings with Miriam. She has a reputation for shrewdness and she's earned it."

He sat cautiously on the edge of his chair. His doggy eyes flickered uneasily. "She explained, as a matter of background, that your father and her father, Mr. Gordon, organized a water company in the Lemon Heights citrus district in 1907."

"I've heard about it," said Miss Jennifer.

"The company had various vicissitudes. . . ." He hissed and stumbled through the word as though a speech had been written out for him and he must stick to it. ". . . uh . . . various troubles which ended finally in Mr. Gordon buying up all the outstanding shares, including Mr. Murdock's, your father's."

"I don't recall the details," said Miss Jennifer.

Mr. Dewel swallowed nervously. "Mr. Gordon was a forceful and impatient man. Almost—ah—ruthless. He obtained the water shares in any manner he judged quickest: by offering a price or, if that failed, by intimidation, threats to cut off water to the groves and even—perhaps even by arson. By burning other people's orchards." He wiped his forehead with a blue-bordered handkerchief. He seemed to be working hard at his speech.

Miss Rachel thought him a very queer little man. She asked, "Are you representing someone's interests in all this?"

"No . . . not at all. I'm a friend of Mrs. Hamilton's. I'm acting only for her."

"You're a friend of Miriam's," she echoed incredulously, "and she sent you to tell us her father committed arson?"

"Wait. Mrs. Hamilton knew nothing of her father's methods. She assumes no responsibility for them. She was a child then, an infant. Recently she has found, in some of her father's old documents, evidence that—well, to be brief, that she owes several people quite a bit of money. Not legally, you understand; not in any way the law defines. But morally. Morally she owes you two ladies, as Mr. Murdock's heirs, and some other people, too, the money her father fleeced out of them."

He was wheezing, as though the speech were over-long and the delivery tedious. There was a twitching place on one of his chins and a frost of sweat on his upper lip.

"She sent you to prepare us? How much will it be?" asked Miss Jennifer, always practical.

"No one knows." He gave her a vague stare. "Perhaps quite an amount. Mrs. Hamilton is working out the exact sum. That's why she wishes you to visit her at her home."

He had slipped it in neatly, almost in the nature of an anticlimax after the rigmarole about the defects of Mr. Gordon. For a moment Miss Jennifer seemed not to understand.

Miss Rachel recalled Miriam's house. It looked exactly like an exclusive country hotel and she always got lost in it the moment she went inside. Every maid had a new face. There were carpets like a deep fur on all the floors and the chandeliers were galaxies of stars. That was Miriam's house. It had thirty-six rooms, not counting the enclosed patio.

"And why on earth," Miss Jennifer was saying, "should we have to go to Miriam's home to get our money?"

"She—ah—she wishes to clear up the debts with a little ceremony."

"Fiddle-faddle," said Miss Jennifer. "Miriam never did anything with ceremony in her life."

He had begun suddenly to look frightened. "Indeed, Miss Jennifer. And you especially, Miss Rachel. She wishes that you would come."

"And why especially me?" asked Miss Rachel, watching him.

He corrected himself quickly. "Did I say that? Of course you're equally desired, both of you, and equally welcome."

"I don't think I'll go," Miss Jennifer decided. "Miriam can just slip our money into an envelope while the ceremony's going on."

"Of course," Miss Rachel said thoughtfully, "it's very nice at Miriam's. It's lovely there."

"Lovely" wasn't the word for the vast impersonality of Miriam's establishment; "baronial" was more suitable; "institutional" even better. Miss Jennifer edged her chair about in a movement of suspicion.

"Rachel, we aren't going anywhere! Positively not, in this heat, at the end of summer, with our nerves in rags!"

"You can sit in Miriam's patio and drink iced tea with limes in it," said Miss Rachel, "or sit and look at motion pictures in her air-conditioned projection room, or swim in her pool."

Miss Jennifer, who hadn't worn a bathing suit since they

stopped being connected to long black stockings, made a sound like a cork popping. "I refuse . . ." she began. "I just positively refuse. . . ."

"I think I'll go," said Miss Rachel.

Mr. Dewel let out a long breath and settled back in his chair. He fanned himself with the handkerchief. He seemed very much like a salesman who had just made a last splendid effort and put over a deal and doesn't quite believe yet that the thing really happened. He was most definitely, in Miss Rachel's opinion, a very odd person.

"When does she want us?" she asked him.

"Not me!" cried Miss Jennifer.

"Me, then," said Miss Rachel smoothly.

"Right away. As soon as possible. Do you have a car? No? Then I'll drive you down. I'll call tomorrow. It should be about a two-hour trip. Shall we make it one o'clock?"

"And no preparation whatever . . ." sputtered Jennifer.

"You aren't going," Miss Rachel reminded. "I'll be ready at one, Mr. Dewel. You understand, don't you, that I'll have to take my cat? She won't let anyone else feed her."

"Cats . . . anything!" breathed Mr. Dewel. He seemed enormously relieved without being very happy about it. "And now, I think, you have a message for me from Mrs. Hamilton?"

Miss Rachel gave him the letter.

He tore it open exactly where it had been pasted, but in the state of nervous relief he seemed to be undergoing, Miss Rachel doubted if he would have noticed something as crude as chewing gum. He took out the slip of note paper first and looked at it and a sudden shade of grimness came into his high-colored face. Then he shook the envelope and the seeds must have slipped into his palm.

He sat looking into his hand for a little space of silence. Then, without speaking, he let the seeds slide into a coat pocket. He hadn't at any time displayed them so that Miss Rachel or Miss Jennifer could see them. He stood up and bowed again; his chins wobbled and the wrinkles appeared briefly across his vest.

He's disappointed, Miss Rachel thought. Something about those seeds or the note wasn't up to expectation. I wonder why on earth Miriam should have sent him three seeds of wisteria, to be given to him if he asked for the letter? She waited, hoping that Mr. Dewel would offer a word of explanation.

He didn't. He began edging toward the hall. "Until tomorrow then."

Miss Rachel's cat, Samantha, black as a midnight sky, came into the doorway from the hall at about the time Mr. Dewel was backing through it. She watched Mr. Dewel's passing with distaste, not being given to friendliness with strangers. He made an awkward move toward petting her and she slid nimbly away.

"Good night," Miss Rachel said; and he had vanished.

Miss Jennifer gave him time to reach the sidewalk before she let forth her opinions in a flood. She thought Miriam must have lost her mind and Mr. Dewel was a fool. She also suspected him of having been drinking. Didn't Rachel?

Miss Rachel innocently denied any acquaintance—even smelling acquaintance—with liquor. "I thought Mr. Dewel was a queer little man. Not a fool though. He seemed to go through a lot of labored thinking." She was remembering his long look at the wisteria seeds.

Miss Jennifer began to clip threads on her embroidered scarf with an air of finality. "We've such a lot to do to get ready to go. Packing. Locking up the house. And we mustn't forget the milkman."

"I thought you weren't going."

"I've changed my mind. It's cool up there and if Miriam's gone crazy some of her relatives—even distant ones like us—ought to know." Miss Jennifer finished the clipping and walked righteously upstairs to bed.

Miss Rachel remained to let the cat out and to stand on the porch, looking at the lights of Los Angeles in the distance below. Their house was on a hill, a very proper hill with a nice view but beside it Miriam's heights were mountains, Miriam's vistas even reached the sea.

Miss Rachel, thoughtful in the dark, made up her mind about a few things. About Mr. Dewel for instance. Mr. Dewel had been afraid she wouldn't come, which must mean that Miriam's instructions had been explicit that she should. Miss Rachel had no illusion that anyone, at any time, had bested her father in a business deal. The whole story about the water shares was, therefore, an elaborate lie. A lie to get her to Miriam's.

The three wisteria seeds would seem to have been Mr. Dewel's strange reward for a job well done.

# CHAPTER TWO

HERBERT GORDON, Miriam's father, had come to California from Maine in 1890. He was already beginning to show signs of the avaricious shrewdness which was to mark him in later life. Some said that he had been involved in a land dispute in the Arizona territory on the way out. He walked with a slight limp which might have been the effect of a bullet wound and it was noted that he never went into a real estate deal without first knowing that he had the upper hand as far as money was concerned, being sure of his water rights, and making friends with the sheriff.

After some years of speculation in and about Los Angeles (then just opening its eyes after its long sleep under the dons) his fancy was taken by the possibilities of some of the wilder sections of Orange County. People were beginning to be interested in citrus culture; frost was a problem in certain sections but not in those parts on which Mr. Gordon had his eye. With the help of a distant relative in Los Angeles—Mr. Murdock, no less—he acquired some thousand or so acres in the western hills. Eventually some of this land, when cleared and planted, was to rise in value to almost three thousand dollars an acre. Herbert Gordon didn't know this but he smelled profit and hung on.

Somewhere at about this time he married a half-Spanish girl, of good family and bad temper, who gave him Miriam. His wife died in 1914.

Gordon himself, knowing his health was failing, took stock in 1926 and discovered that he was leaving his daughter some million and a half dollars in property and water shares.

Miriam had combined her mother's patrician temper with her father's plebeian bullheadedness; and after Gordon's death she carried on much as he had, which is to say she ruled with an iron hand and made enemies and crushed them down with the power of her wealth. Her empire waxed and grew land-heavy and staggered into the thirty's and there bogged down with a threat of disintegration. Still sure of herself, Miriam made furious demands on banks and found the officials there snappish and as lost as she. There must have been a time about then when Miriam looked at disaster and found it terrible.

In the autumn of 1932 she married Mr. John Flanders, who had seen the crash coming and had prudently turned his stocks, bonds, and cattle into cash. He saved Miriam's empire for her (the groves were beginning to be sprinkled here and there with experimental plantings of avocados), built her a house on a hill, and had then the grace to die.

He had been an exceptionally homely man and there was the suspicion among Miriam's relatives (notably Miss Jennifer) that she was more relieved than stricken over his going. He had left, unfortunately, more of a legacy than money. He had had a son by a previous marriage, a tall leggy boy called Rick, who in 1934 was fifteen. Rick had enough of his father's ugliness to give his face character and enough of his dead mother's softness to give it sensitivity. He liked mechanical things: motors, cameras, pumps; and he kept out of Miriam's way by spending most of his free time in the barns and garages.

It was Rick, however, who was the cause of Miriam's meeting Ray Hamilton. Hamilton came over one day to return a bridle Rick had loaned him. He was tall, blond, likable, and easygoing. He owned a section of fairly worthless hilly land to the north of Miriam's sleek acres. He had built a shack amidst the manzanita growth and was living there with his daughter. Once in a while he planted a few orange trees and the rest of the time he did magazine illustrations. He had scant respect for money because it could in no way bring him the thing he wanted. He was on the trail of a painting technique which he hoped would be distinctive enough to make him famous. Fame was his spur; you couldn't talk with him five minutes and not know it. Miss Rachel had felt it as a fire that seemed to scorch him from within.

He had shaken hands with Miriam in exactly the same way he shook hands with her cook. Perhaps less interestedly, since the cook had a jovial and interesting face and Miriam's was cold and self-contained.

Miriam was intrigued with him. He was, for one thing, quite different from Mr. Flanders. He was so good-looking that Miriam was seized with a desire simply to sit and look at him for the rest of her life. Just how she carried on her conquest was a secret, but they were married the next summer and the Misses Murdock went to the wedding. Rick was there, scrubbed and lanky and somehow lonesome among all the others. Miss Rachel, seeing a crouched shape behind some drapery, found Mr. Hamilton's little girl. She had white silky skin, brown eyes, a mouth that seemed ready to ask a great many questions. "I'm Sharon," she had whispered.

Miss Rachel had given her a hanky for her tears.

In 1940 Ray Hamilton announced that he had a job doing sketches of the war in France for a New York paper. If he wangled the job with the help of Miriam's money, as some said he had, it was with her express displeasure also, for she wanted him home to look at. There must have been some bitter arguments before he sailed.

In France, in the last days at Dunkirk, Ray Hamilton was killed.

Miriam now had two stepchildren, almost two million dollars in property, a house with thirty-six rooms, and a mind boiling with angry bewilderment. She could not understand why Ray Hamilton had chosen to leave her for the battlefields of Europe nor why he should have been killed there before she could coax him back home. There were times when rage and despair and frustration made her want to murder, one by one, every person with whom she came in contact. There were other times when she longed to kill herself. She emerged gradually into a state of repression, of inward torture and outward rudeness, which alienated all who knew her.

"Don't you think there's something terribly wrong with Miriam?" Miss Jennifer had asked at about this stage.

Miss Rachel had glanced up from a recipe for sherry mousse (not that there was any chance of Jennifer allowing her to bring home the sherry) and answered: "She's afraid."

"Afraid?"

"Of life. She doesn't understand why it must include dying." Miss Rachel had frowned at her recipe. "Nor why, I think, money can't buy immortality."

A prophetic remark; Miss Rachel was to remember it a long time afterward.

Mr. Dewel appeared at one o'clock with a clean, shabby, and somewhat asthmatic sedan. He assisted Miss Rachel and Miss Jennifer into the rear seat and placed the cat's basket between them. He put their suitcases into the front seat with himself. Today, Miss Rachel noted, he smelled of Listerine, peppermint, and rum. Mr. Dewel, she thought, seemed omnivorous and impartial in his taste. He drove carefully, not talking much. The back of his neck had the unexpectedly bare look that so many fat men's have; and the fringe of hair under his hat, she saw, was touched with gray. She wanted to ask him what he had done with the wisteria seeds and knew that she must not. Morally, as Mr. Dewel would say, she hadn't seen them.

They left Los Angeles and took a broad highway skirting the beaches and came, after an hour or so, into the warm dry uplands of Orange County. The sky was very blue that day, gauzy at the edges with the haze common to California. The orange trees, now that they were in the citrus belt, were at first like a low forest on all sides of them and then, as they climbed higher, like a carpet laid out upon the land. The chugging car kept a firm grip on the road and they whirled up and up until they were above the haze, looking out across it to the Santa Ana Mountains, brown as a coyote's flank; and the valleys between were one vast green sparkle like a sea.

The few homes on these heights were big, a preparation for the vastness of Miriam's. They came to a last curve, a last swing up into the sky, and there it was. In the first moment of seeing it Miss Rachel was always conscious of the feeling that it must be a sanitarium or a museum or an exclusive inn, that it was too big to be simply a home. Mr. Dewel chose the moment to announce unnecessarily that they had arrived.

The graveled driveway climbed through a border of delphiniums and pink roses to the side of the house. Mr. Dewel stopped under the porte-cochere and assisted them to get out. With the handle of the cat's basket over her arm and Miss Jennifer at her heels, Miss Rachel went into Miriam's hall. The maid who came to greet them was waxy-faced, plump, polite. She asked if they'd excuse Mrs. Hamilton at the moment; she was busy; and would they care to see their rooms?

They went up, Mr. Dewel carrying suitcases, into the utter stillness of the upper floor. The quiet of Miriam's house had never made Miss Rachel think of its excellent insulation—only of the dead stillness of a tomb. She didn't like it; she was too used to the creaking blowziness of her old house in Los Angeles.

The maid opened doors for them and Mr. Dewel deposited the luggage and excused himself and went away. Miss Rachel's room had walls of pink flecked with gold, a taffeta bed in cerise, vast fluffy rugs the color of canary feathers. After the grim Victorianism of her mahogany at home, she felt a little giddy. She felt like peeking into a mirror to see if she were really seventy and wearing lavender taffeta.

She was.

Investigating hers and Jennifer's mutual bath, she found Jennifer there looking with disapproval at a sunken black tub set among mirrors etched with fishes and kelp. She knew that Jennifer would never bathe in a contraption like that. "You can borrow the cook's, every afternoon," she suggested.

"I shall itch," Miss Jennifer threatened, "and I'll scratch in public, if we aren't gone in a day or two."

"I'll blush for you," said Miss Rachel, unmoved. She saw Jennifer's room through the open door. It had a Byzantine lushness, purple and white, which suited Miss Jennifer's angular primness about as well as an ermine nightgown. There were rugs Jennifer would fear to crush with her sensible shoes; there was a bed in which she would get lost. Miss Rachel sighed. Miriam was getting a little frenzied in her search for ways to spend money.

"Well, we can freshen up." Miss Jennifer ran water into a black basin and dipped her fingers gingerly. "I wonder when the ceremony's coming off. Mr. Dewel seemed vague. I'm going to ask Miriam the minute I see her."

They let the cat out into the rooms and shut her in when they left. Undecided where to find Miriam, they wandered about the lower floor. They inspected one room which seemed to be a bar and game room, another given to antiques and a display of old glass, a third barren save for a grand piano all alone in splendor. Then from an open door they heard voices and the tick of a typewriter, which they followed.

The terrace was on the side opposite the drive, sheltered to the south by a mass of shrubbery. It was floored with yellow brick, fenced with an iron grillwork, knee-high, in an intricate design somewhat like a flower. There was a view of the flank of Miriam's hill, the swimming pool and terraces, the great valley, the green stretches of distance, and a far winking sparkle that must be the Pacific surf. The winds bore the odor of orange blossoms and sage on the bare hills. Miss Rachel, stepping out ahead of Jennifer, saw a wrought-iron table near at hand. From it rose politely the figures of two men: Mr. Joe Dewel and another. In front of a typewriter, and with her face turned toward them, was Sharon Hamilton.

Mr. Dewel was bowing, smiling his uncertain smile, murmuring something about a brother. Miss Rachel inspected the other man. He was thin where Mr. Dewel was fat; he had none of Mr. Dewel's wobblings, physical or otherwise, but the resemblance between them struck her. Eyes, she decided. Eyes that in

Mr. Dewel were weepy like an airedale's and in his brother had the quickness of a terrier's. His name was Bart. Mr. Bart Dewel. While Miss Rachel nodded acknowledgment she decided that the flair for wearing sport clothes in loud colors had here reached its extreme: Mr. Bart Dewel's slacks were burgundy, his shirt powder-blue, his jacket yellow-orange. He wore clothes well, being thin and muscular. He was somewhere over thirty-five, perhaps not so old as forty. He was chewing a toothpick. He had a distinct air of belonging where he was.

Sharon, of course, they knew. She still had the pale silky skin, the big eyes, the mouth with its odd look of wanting to ask a question. She was a very pretty girl in Miss Rachel's opinion, but too thin. She was wearing a plain black dress without any hint of color. She had worn black since her father's death; there was a grim, unhappy note in this long grieving that didn't sit well with her youth, with the fresh beauty she had, like that of a flower. She got up as they approached and held out a hand.

"Are you looking for Miriam? She'll be out shortly. There's some question of a change in fertilizers she's trying to settle with the foremen." She came close and took their hands in hers. "I'm so awfully glad you're here. It's been ages."

She kissed them gently.

"You should visit us once in a while in town and shop a bit and see some shows," Miss Rachel said, trying not to be too obvious about not noticing the black dress. "We'd be so glad to have an excuse to run about a bit."

"I'll do that," she said, though her eyes didn't promise it. "Sometime soon."

"Sharon's all tied up now," said Bart Dewel, shifting the toothpick. "She's trying to be a writer. She's got an idea for a book. Sounds like a good one too."

He laughed easily and something came into Sharon's eyes: a reserve, a blotting out of friendliness. She said: "It's just a pastime. I write one day and tear it all up the next. Would you like something to drink after your drive?"

Miss Jennifer wanted tea. Miss Rachel said she wanted a lemonade and then by wriggling her eyebrows behind Jennifer's back she conveyed to Sharon that it really might as well be a cocktail. Sharon went away to find a maid. They sat down with the two Mr. Dewels.

When Sharon returned she began putting the typewriter into its case. Mr. Bart Dewel chewed his toothpick and watched her. Once when Mr. Joe Dewel thought no one was looking he took a quick drink from a flask. Afterward he seemed considerably heartened.

Miss Rachel's drink came and proved to be a well-disguised old-fashioned. There was more than enough tea for all, and so Mr. Bart Dewel said he'd have some. He let Sharon put two lumps of sugar into his cup. "Sweets from the sweet," he said.

She didn't look up.

The shadows of afternoon had begun to creep across the terrace; there was a hint of cooler air rising from the valley, of haze over the sun. All at once Miss Rachel was conscious of a remarkable thing.

There was a human hand sticking through the wall of shrubbery at her right.

# CHAPTER THREE

SHE FELT an electric jangle of nerves; and then she saw the hand move and realized at the same instant that there was an opening in the hedge, thinly concealed by a few twigs of new growth, and that Rick Flanders was coming through. He had, she remembered, a quiet way of approaching other people; caution, perhaps, bred of the years he had spent with Miriam's unpredictable temper. He had still the likable ugliness, the sensitive eyes; but there was an adult hardness to his body, and his quiet manner had more of purpose in it than before. Miss Rachel recalled that he had served in the Army and had seen action in the Solomons and had suffered a shrapnel wound in the lung. He must be somewhere near twenty-seven. His father had left him some small independent income and Miss Rachel had understood that Miriam paid him for his work for her as she would a foreman. The home that his father's money had built had never been anyone's but Miriam's.

He seemed to find something of interest in Mr. Bart Dewel.

"Come on over, Rick," Sharon called when she saw him. "Here are some old friends come for a visit. You remember Miss Rachel and Miss Jennifer."

He came gravely to shake their hands. He wore faded denim and smelled of motor oil and hay. He nodded to Joe Dewel and just looked Bart Dewel in the eye. "It's good to see you again," he said to Miss Rachel and Miss Jennifer. "Excuse my looks, will you? I've been doing some repairs on a tractor."

"Have some tea," said Sharon. She seemed a little brighter, a little easier in manner since Rick had come. "One lump, Rick?"

"That's plenty." He took the tea as if he wished to humor her.

"Fill mine again, darling," said Bart Dewel.

She ignored the touch of his hand under the teacup.

"I'm looking for Miriam," said Rick. "Have you seen her?"

"She's inside somewhere." Sharon turned to the house as though Miriam should be coming out. "She's later than she thought she'd be. Wait. Here she is. No, it's Mrs. Krythe."

Mrs. Krythe was a wisp of a woman with fuzzy faded hair, a grayish complexion, a dress that someone larger must have handed down to her, and an air of being out of place on Miriam's terrace and knowing it. She had a low, wavering voice. "I'm lost, I guess. I thought I'd taken the right turn to reach the drive, but I didn't. There are so many rooms, and the halls confused me." She made a bewildered gesture with one hand which, Miss Rachel noted, held a roll of samples of chintz. "I came to match the draperies in the sunroom, you know, and to measure the divan there for a slip cover. I—I guess I should have asked Mrs. Hamilton for a map." She laughed at her small joke, looking from one face to another.

"I'll show you the way." Sharon stood up from behind the table. "Your chintz looks very attractive. May I see it?"

Sharon held out her hand. Mrs. Krythe could not have intended to be as rude as her actions made her seem. She must not have heard Sharon's question, for she had turned her back and started quickly toward the door. Sharon shrugged and went after her. The roll of chintz, bright with color, shone with a metallic luster as Mrs. Krythe carried it into the hall.

"She has a shop in the village," Bart Dewel said idly. "Notions and stuff. Hey, she's dropped something at the door. See it shine?" He got out of his chair, walked leisurely to the door, and there stooped to pick up a reflection of the metallic glitter which had seemed to be in the cloth. "Good night! What do you call this thing?"

He brought it to the table and Miss Jennifer and Rick and Joe Dewel bent to look. Miss Rachel was trying to recall where she had seen such an article before. "I believe," she told him, "that it's an upholsterer's needle. It's large, in order to sew through heavy materials and padding. Mrs. Krythe would use something like that, I suppose, in her work." Though she wondered privately if such a length of steel was necessary in the making of slip covers.

The sunlight glittered on it as on a blade. There was a moment of curious silence.

"I ought to run after her, I guess," said Bart Dewel, shifting his toothpick thoughtfully. "No, on second thought she'll probably be back again tomorrow. And anyway, she must have more than one of the things."

"For some reason," said Miss Jennifer worriedly, "it looks like an ugly and dangerous thing to me. Doesn't it to you?"

"Hmmm?" he said, thrusting his hands into the pockets of the orange-yellow jacket. "No. It's just a needle." The powder-blue shirt cast a reflection on his chin that made him look vaguely unshaven. His quick eyes seemed to have grown suddenly mask-like. "Only . . . speaking of needles . . . 'Needles and pins, needles and pins, when a man marries his troubles begin.'"

"'Trouble begins,'" corrected Miss Jennifer. "Then it rhymes."

He didn't seem to be listening.

"Are you married, Mr. Dewel?" Miss Jennifer asked him practically.

"Not yet." There was some dry amusement in the flick of his eye toward Rick Flanders. "No. Someday soon, perhaps."

Rick said, "Excuse me. I'm going to try to find Miriam." He went off into the house.

When Sharon returned she looked about as if seeking him. Bart Dewel smirked at her. "Am I invited to stay for dinner again, darling?"

"Certainly." She made it sound like the ready courtesy she kept for strangers. "And you too, Joe. If you'd like."

Mr. Joe Dewel, who had preserved a steady and, Miss Rachel suspected, an increasingly alcoholic silence, nodded absently. His eyes had followed the shadow on the terrace as though the approach of night were wearying and worrisome. "I say, though, Miriam's apt to get tired of us."

"Of course she won't. Shall we go inside? It's growing quite cool here."

They went inside and found a thin yellow-headed boy talking to Rick in the hall. He turned toward the group a face full of questioning anxiety. He had freckles on a fair skin, clothes discreetly patched, long legs as awkward as a colt's.

Rick said, "This is Jerry Krythe. He says he was supposed to pick up his mother here and he can't find her."

"She's gone," said Sharon. "She walked away. You should have met her on the road coming up."

"Never saw her," said the boy in a voice deepened with worry. "Could she have come back here after something?"

They must have all thought of the needle—all save Sharon, who hadn't seen it lying on the table on the terrace.

"I think," said Miss Rachel smoothly, "that your mother may have returned to find something she dropped in leaving. I'll get it for you." She slipped out quickly onto the terrace before any of the others had moved.

It seemed that in the moment of their being indoors the day had turned to twilight. Though the sun still struck the tops of the trees beyond the terrace, the feeling of dusk had increased: the haze was gray and the wind biting. She walked to the table and looked down upon its surface. At her foot was Sharon's typewriter in its case, but the needle, the long steel needle, was gone.

There was an odd quiet over the dinner table. Miriam had sent word by the waxy-faced maid to say that she was still too busy to join them. Rick was off helping Jerry Krythe to look for his mother. Sharon wore a manner of listening and worrying, shared by Miss Jennifer, who hadn't liked the fact of the needle's being gone. The Dewel brothers and Miss Rachel, however, preserved their original manner: Bart sly and gay, Joe surreptitiously alcoholic, Miss Rachel pleasantly inclined to giggle. She had found in the past that a giggling little old lady is presumed not to think.

She listened receptively for such scraps as fell concerning the Dewels: that they lived near by in a bachelor establishment, renting what had once been a foreman's house; that they had been friends of Ray Hamilton before they had met Miriam; that Bart Dewel dabbled in real estate from a promotional angle and that Joe Dewel seemed to have no occupation save running errands for Miriam. Bart had never been married. Joe was a widower with a son at Stanford.

Miss Rachel took in these facts and filed them mentally while she sought for an answer to Miriam's evasion of Jennifer and herself. Miriam had wanted them to come here—had wanted Miss Rachel at any rate—and had sent Joe Dewel to bring them. And since their coming Miriam hadn't appeared even long enough to say hello.

The dessert came, a pink sherbet topped with almonds, and thin buttery cookies, and little glasses of port at which Miss Jennifer showed a proper prohibitionist scorn.

"I can't help wondering about Mrs. Krythe," Miss Rachel said with a touch of careful disinterest. "Where she went . . . how she disappeared so quickly."

Joe Dewel assured her that Mrs. Krythe would turn up. No one had ever been lost permanently on Lemon Heights. There was a State Highway Patrol car in the district; if she were in difficulties they'd find her.

When dinner was over Sharon asked if the others wouldn't like to walk out and see if Rick had come. Only Miss Rachel and Bart showed an eagerness to go. They left Miss Jennifer and Joe with after-dinner coffee in what Miriam called her study, a warm and bookish place less baronial than the living room.

Miss Rachel and Bart followed Sharon through the hall to the driveway. Rick had gone with Jerry Krythe in a battered pickup truck; the truck was Jerry's and it had, to Miss Rachel's eye, the same clean and patched look as his clothes. He used it in doing odd jobs for the ranchers. Sharon paused in the drive, looking down at the road, and asked Bart if he'd mind scouting off that way a bit. He didn't leave with any show of willingness; Miss Rachel got the impression that if she herself had been anything less than seventy, grasshopper-frail, and strange to the place, he might have asked her to go instead.

He walked away quickly and the shadowy rim of the hill swallowed him.

Sharon made a face after him. "Now we can talk," she said. "Do you know why Miriam had you come up here?"

"To settle something about the water shares," said Miss Rachel.

"Nonsense. I heard her making that story up out of whole cloth with Joe Dewel. She wanted you to come because she's furious over something she doesn't understand."

"What is it?"

They were walking the grassy strip which paralleled the drive. To their left was a low bank of roses trained on a wire fence and the dark fringe of the grove that covered most of Miriam's hill. To their right was the drive and the high wall of Miriam's house. Ahead were garages and outbuildings painted white, their outlines sharp in the dusk. Sharon turned toward Miss Rachel a face in which anger covered a trace of nervousness.

"There's something queer and revengeful going on and for some insane reason she suspects me."

In the moment of silence that came after Sharon's words Miss Rachel heard the far coughing of a motor on the hill—Jerry Krythe's battered truck perhaps—and the rustle of the wind among the trees. "Tell me about it, all of it," she said.

"There's very little that I know. Miriam has had days recently of not speaking to me, of looking at me as though she loathed me. I couldn't understand why and I couldn't bring myself to ask her. You know how Miriam can be; I wanted to crawl away somewhere out of her sight. Then I found out something about the mischief. Checkers told me."

"I remember about Checkers," said Miss Rachel. "He's very old, and he's worked for Miriam for years. He grows fuchsias for her and she exhibits them. He's almost blind from some accident or other."

"He had an accident with a defective sprayer," Sharon said; her voice was quieter, regretful. "That must have been five years or more ago—about the time Father left for Europe. That's why Miriam took Checkers out of the groves and let him grow flowers. The sprayer should have been repaired."

Miss Rachel wondered that Checkers had asked so little for the damage to his sight.

Sharon went on. "Checkers told me what's been happening to the fuchsias. Here, I'll show you." She had swerved from the grass border by the drive to follow a path that circled the garages and came out into a cleared space before a great barn.

Here it was shadowy and quiet. The sky was fading from the opalescent colors of sunset to a windy bronze; there was a dull light along its western edge that threw an odd glow over the empty corral, the white fence, the high front of the barn. The upper half of the wide heavy barn door was open, showing a cluttered darkness. Sharon pulled at the iron hasp on the lower section, opened it, and they went in.

"Through here," she said.

A small tractor, the one Rick had been working on perhaps, stood facing the door, surrounded by a litter of tools through which they picked their way. In the dim spaces at either side Miss Rachel saw cultivating equipment, sprayers, vast spreads of canvas used in fumigating the trees, canisters and boxes of chemicals, ladders, crates.

Behind the tractor was a second door, divided at shoulder height like the first, and closed. Sharon pulled the upper section open and looked through. Miss Rachel saw that this addition to the barn was a long lath house. Light came in grayly from the sky. There was a smell of moss and wet earth and manure. Fuchsias in pots and in cans crowded the benches and tables which had been built against the walls. The fuchsia blossoms made a show of purple and pink and crimson like a vivid panorama of jewels.

A bent form straightened at the far end of the aisle where lantana and moon vine had tunneled in through the slats, a jungle thicket full of bloom.

"Just me, Checkers," said Sharon. "I've a friend here."

They waited while he came slowly closer.

"Miss Rachel, may I present Checkers? Or have you met before?"

"We've spoken," said Miss Rachel. "I think we differed once about the amount of sand you mix with the loam in a flowerpot."

"He'll show us his prize babies if we're nice, perhaps," said Sharon.

Around sixty, he had a craggy tallness, a seamed, weathery face, a blunt hand which he held out toward her, eyes in which something more than sight had died.

"Pleased to meet you," he said. "Don't see so well. Remember that about the sand though. Heh. You're the lady detective I've heard about."

"I've had a few little successes," said Miss Rachel modestly. "May we really see your fuchsias? They're lovely."

"Sure. Come on. Watch out for puddles, I ain't got all the grit I need for these walks yet. Here. Here's Bonnie Bell."

He reached into a nest of greenery and drew forth a little plant all crimson stars and pearly ruffles.

"You're keeping this one hidden?" asked Sharon quietly.

"Guess I'd better." He turned the pot so that the blossoms

twinkled and then set the plant back among the ferns. "You want to show her what happened to the other?"

"Yes. Quickly. Wait here, Checkers."

Sharon's slim black form ran on ahead, turned right, bent toward a heap of broken pots and rusted gardening tools and bags of manure. She drew from concealment there a little plant which seemed on the first instant to be a duplicate of the one Checkers had just shown them. Then Miss Rachel saw that the crimson stars were curling, the pearly ruffles withered with the touch of death.

# CHAPTER FOUR

"LOOK CLOSELY at the stem," Sharon whispered.

Miss Rachel looked. Almost invisibly the stem had been scored round with something sharp.

"I don't know why Miriam should have thought I'd do it," Sharon said miserably. "But she must have. She loves these fuchsias—as much as she loves anything—and she's collected a lot of blue ribbons and loving cups from the shows." Sharon touched a blossom gently and the wilted petals clung to her hand. "There have been others, Checkers said."

A cold breath seemed to steal up out of the earth to envelop them. Sharon looked at Miss Rachel. "I wonder why she hasn't talked to you yet? Perhaps she's waiting for tonight, for everyone to go or to be in bed. Perhaps she'll get in touch with you then."

"I wonder if she will?" said Miss Rachel. She wondered, too, if she was to have an explanation of the wisteria seeds for Mr. Dewel.

"I'll put this away and we'll go back to the house." Sharon concealed the little plant under the heap of tools. They admired a few of Checkers's treasures on the way to the door. The yard in front of the barn had the unreal dimensions of twilight: the white boards of the fence seemed close, substantial, the trees behind them a vague line of darkness. The graveled path answered their footsteps with a ghostly crunching.

In the house there was news of a sort. Rick had been in to say that he and Jerry hadn't found Mrs. Krythe but that the boy had remembered some friends she might have visited, taking a path through the groves, and had driven there to see. Bart had returned from the errand Sharon had sent him on, saying he hadn't met anyone. He was waiting to pay his respects to Sharon before he and Joe left for home.

In thanking her for the dinner he tried to hold her hand, but Sharon put her hand into the pocket of her black skirt.

When the two Dewels had gone in Joe's asthmatic car Sharon made Rick join them for bridge. He had changed, for his delayed dinner, to a dark well-cut suit which made him look leaner, older, more reserved. He had combed a somewhat wild look from his hair. His quiet adult manner concealed almost completely the lonely, lost expression he had had as a boy; there was just a trace of it when he glanced at Sharon, as though she were the only thing he weren't sure of, the one enigma left in his world. He played bridge well, but there was the thought in Miss Rachel's mind that he did it to please her and Jennifer and Sharon—Sharon perhaps most—and not because cards held any interest for him.

At midnight Miss Rachel roused to the buzz of the telephone by her bed. She sat up, pulled on the light, and lifted the receiver to hear the metallic bluntness of Miriam's voice.

Miriam went through a brief process of hoping Miss Rachel was well and enjoying her visit. Then she got down to business. "I'm sorry that I caused you the trouble of coming up here. I had a problem which was worrying me a little and I thought you might help."

"I should be glad to do anything I can," Miss Rachel offered. "If you'll explain——"

"No, no," said Miriam. "It isn't necessary now. I'm going to handle things myself."

"And the ceremony about the money?" said Miss Rachel.

"Well. . . I'll make you and Jennifer out a check. For a hundred or so. How would that do? There really isn't anything coming from the water shares. I made that up as a cover for the real story, and to get you up here."

Miss Rachel felt anger rise, to prickle her scalp and set her throat tingling. "Of course you won't make out a check. I'm not really for hire, you know."

"I know. Just a hobby. Well, if you really . . ."

Miss Rachel looked toward the door to the bath and saw Jennifer there, huddled and sleepy in a gray flannel nightgown. "What are you doing at this hour?" Jennifer yawned. "Who is it on the phone?"

Miss Rachel put the phone briskly in its cradle and got out of bed. Her cat, black as a goblin, rose from the blanket beside her and stretched and stared at the light questioningly.

"I was talking to Miriam," said Miss Rachel. "I didn't finish. I'm going to her room. There are some things, as you would put it, Jennifer, which no lady would say over the phone and I intend to say them."

"To Miriam?"

"Since you're the victim of her inconsideration as much as I, you may come along."

"I don't understand. You seem so angry about something."

Miss Rachel jerked at a fur slipper. "I've never been angrier."

"But the money Miriam wants us to have, Rachel. Isn't that pretty good of her, offering us that?"

"There isn't any money, a fact which I rather suspected from the beginning. Miriam got us up here with a lie about the water shares. She had a problem, a puzzle—I gathered, perhaps, a job of snooping—and she thought I might handle things for her. Now she's decided to do it alone."

Miss Jennifer came back with unexpected vehemence: "If that's why she brought us up, Rachel, I have something to say too."

"You don't know the words," Miss Rachel pointed out. "I do. I used to listen to Father when he couldn't find his shirt studs."

Miss Jennifer flamed. "Father wouldn't——"

"Father would too. I don't know why you choose to remember him as such a sissy. Are you coming, Jennifer?" Miss Rachel had put on a woolly pink robe over her gown.

Miss Jennifer moved toward her uncertainly, the folds of flannel dragging like a collapsed tent. Part of Miss Jennifer's moral code consisted of getting herself up as unattractively as possible for bed; she had discarded a knitted cap only recently and after long haggling from Rachel. "Perhaps, though, for the sake of dignity, of keeping a calm manner——"

"I'm in no mood for a calm anything. When I've finished saying what I have to say to Miriam Hamilton I'll think about dignity." She swept out into the hall and Jennifer and the cat came hurrying after.

The hall had a night light above the stairs. Miss Rachel hurried along carpets which quenched every sound, turned right, found Miriam's white-and-gold door, and rapped.

There was no answering stir, no step, no rustle of garment.

She pushed the door open and found nothing inside but

darkness and silence. For an instant she stood there puzzled. She had taken for granted the fact that Miriam had called from her own bedroom.

In the glow from the hall she saw Miriam's bed set in its alcove, vast under brocade and lace, and undisturbed by any sleeper. The chaise in the center of the room was empty. The wide floor was marked with faint oblongs of light from a bank of windows; outside were the feathery tops of shrubs, a pale sky beginning to show moonlight through a gauzy trace of fog. Miss Rachel took a few steps into the room, looked into the alcove containing the bed, then turned toward Jennifer.

Jennifer had come in; she was standing on Miriam's silky carpet as though rooted in it. Miss Rachel noted with surprise that her mouth was open and her chin shaking. She seemed to be trying to point to something across the room.

Miss Rachel turned slowly to look again at the bank of windows and the night.

The tips of shrubbery moved as a bobbing shape came through them. A small light, rising with the object, illumined the upper portion with a yellow, matchlike glow. For an instant, while all the house seemed suddenly to quieten, Miss Rachel had the crazy impression that she was looking at a dead dwarf.

The cat growled, a ruffled uneasy sound. Jennifer screeched: "Rachel, do you see it?"

"Hush," said Rachel. "Wait, and don't move."

The thing bobbed closer to the pane, touched the glass with a soft bump, hung there as if looking in. Blue eyes met Miss Rachel's, eyes as shallow as a saucer, gleaming as porcelain. From a broken place in the head a red sticky stain had run. The yellow hair was dull, matted. The whole thing had a crushed, soiled, indefinably buried-and-dug-up look that was revolting.

"What is it?" moaned Jennifer.

"It's a doll," said Miss Rachel. "A very queer doll." She trembled with a chill; she felt as though something horrible had tried to reach through the window to touch her.

"I'm going to scream!"

"Be quiet!"

Miss Jennifer proceeded to choke on the beginning of hysterics and Miss Rachel put her without ceremony into the hall. Then she closed the door and stood with her back to it and watched the hanging thing outside.

The little light moved with the gyrations of the doll as if it were fastened to it. Though the trunk was in shadow, Miss Rachel judged from the size of the face that it was a very large doll, perhaps two feet tall or more. The big quiet room, the lighted sky beyond, gave the effect of a stage with a single marionette upon it. The staring face moved up and down, slowly, against the glass; the red running stain had a gleam like that of blood.

"Dolls don't bleed," Miss Rachel said to herself out loud in the dark.

Even as she said it the figure dropped suddenly from sight.

Miss Rachel ran to the window, looked down into blackness. Then she bolted out into the hall.

Miss Jennifer, meanwhile, had had time to collect her wits and to do some thinking. What she thought about must have been the course of Rachel's future action. She was ready. She seized the tail of Miss Rachel's woolly robe and clung to it. There followed then a tug of war at which the cat was an interested spectator.

"Let *go!*" cried Miss Rachel, wriggling furiously.

"No, you don't!" said Jennifer. "Not in your slippers and gown. It wouldn't be proper and people would say things."

Miss Rachel looked at her in stark disbelief. "Do you mean that with the insane stuff going on here anyone would look twice at me in a nightgown? Don't be an idiot! I've got to run and see who's doing tricks with that dreadful doll! Leave me go!"

"If you'll come to your room," said Jennifer, hanging on, "and put on some clothes and take a flashlight and let me come along too——"

"To hold me back at a crucial moment!"

"To keep you from getting killed—you can go," Miss Jennifer finished. "Otherwise, not."

In the defense of propriety Miss Jennifer was a lion. The struggle ended with Miss Rachel's surrender. She threw clothes on herself in the bedroom while Jennifer, gimlet-eyed, did the same in the other room with both doors to the bath open. The cat explored the bed sleepily and then, sensing that Miss Rachel had prowling on her mind, leaped down to wait beside the door.

"Not you!" Miss Rachel scolded. The cat closed her eyes and mewed.

Miss Jennifer came in wearing a long coat and carrying a flashlight. "No, I think we'd better take the cat. She might warn of something creeping in the dark."

"She'll creep off herself to catch mice."

"We'll take her anyway."

They went cautiously down through silent halls to the terrace.

A dark figure rose from beside the table where Sharon had poured tea that afternoon. Miss Jennifer promptly turned the flashlight on it. Miss Rachel saw a lean gray man, very tall, with a narrow face in which suave eyes, slightly pouched, regarded Jennifer's light. He wore a well-cut business suit under a windproof coat. A briefcase lay on the table.

He flicked a cigarette away over the edge of the terrace. "Hello," he said. He had a low, casual voice. "Looking for something?"

They were struck dumb with surprise. Finally Miss Rachel said, "We're Mrs. Hamilton's cousins. I don't believe we know you."

A twitch of a smile crossed his lips. "The Misses Murdock? I've heard Miriam speak of you. I'm Miriam's office boy. I believe she calls me an estate manager. Braudryck's the name." He bowed toward them. His bow had none of Mr. Dewel's wobblings; it was courtly and winning.

Miss Rachel's mind knitted up a whole fabric of fact concerning Mr. Braudryck out of things Miriam had said about him. He was a good attorney with a flourishing practice in Santa Ana. He handled Miriam's legal affairs and he had, so far, kept her ruthless dealings from the attention of a court.

"Miriam and I have been talking out here," he went on. "She's gone inside for a wrap and for a thermos of something warm to drink. I told her that I wasn't in the habit of discussing business in the pitch-dark outdoors at midnight . . . but you know Miriam. She seemed to think that something needed to be quite secret."

It was more than an explanation. It was a hint that they should run along.

"Indeed," stammered Miss Jennifer.

"I should like to see Miriam for a moment," said Miss Rachel.

He shrugged his eyebrows. "She's inside."

"Unfortunately we didn't meet her."

He had taken on a look of suddenly thinking about something else. "Perhaps you could tell me—was there a Mrs. Krythe here this afternoon? She's a sort of middle-aged, timid person. She has a drapery and drygoods shop in the village."

"Yes, we saw her," Miss Rachel told him. "Why?"

"Hmmm? Oh. Just wondering." He looked ironic and secretive.

"Perhaps you'll tell us something in return," said Miss Rachel smoothly. "We were wondering which windows were those of Miriam's room."

"Her room?" His face relaxed, grew blank. "I really don't know. At the end of the terrace somewhere, past the cypress, I think. I couldn't be sure."

"We'll look there." She began to move away, the cat at her heels.

"Why?" asked Mr. Braudryck.

"Hmmm?" said Miss Rachel. "Oh. Just wondering."

They moved away to the muffled sound of his laughter. He seemed to be enjoying Miss Rachel's spiteful mimicry.

They found a gate in the low iron railing and went through. The yellow spot of Jennifer's light moved ahead to show a row of stiff little trees (the cypresses Mr. Braudryck had mentioned), a tangle of honeysuckle on a framework of timbers, and amaryllis, pink bells in the midst of ferns. There was little sign of cultivation here, as though the efforts of the gardener had been directed where display would be seen, at the front of the house and along the drive. Fallen cypress twigs were brittle underfoot. The ferns were overgrown, the honeysuckle rampant. The cat frolicked with her shadow, liking the rustle she made. Miss Rachel regarded the stout beams of the arbor and the windows directly above.

"This is the spot," she whispered to Jennifer. "The arbor would be a concealment. He could thrust the doll up through the vine."

"You don't know that it's a he."

"A good point." Miss Rachel was silent for a moment. Then she took Jennifer's wrist and caused the yellow circle to crawl up the outer wall of the arbor. The windows above were black, empty. She brought the light down to explore the interior where broken places and torn shreds of vine showed. "Nothing to prove," she said, "that anyone stood here. The earth's too solid, too gravelly. Let's scout a bit. We might find something."

"I'm not really anxious to see that awful doll again. I'd rather just go back to bed." Miss Jennifer shivered. "It's sort of dewy and clammy and—and silent out here."

"Yes, I miss the traffic too." Miss Rachel was listening with her white head on one side as though the tune the crickets played intrigued her. "Bugs don't count of course. And the mockingbirds have a ghostly sweetness that's rather weird. A few streetcars going by would help."

"Rachel, if you're going to make fun——"

"I'm not making fun." She slipped back the way they had come until she could see the terrace. Mr. Braudryck was still alone in the dim moonlight, smoking. His figure was dark and erect; there was a hint of irritation at Miriam's delay.

She went back to Jennifer. "Perhaps it would be more tactful to use another entrance. Let's find the kitchen." They circled the arbor and found a path almost concealed in a riot of zinnias. The path ended in a paved space before the garages. A car that was probably Mr. Braudryck's waited there; it was, like him, gray and immaculate and expensive. Samantha touched an investigative nose to its running board. A light burned by a screened entry; another light inside showed them Miriam's service porch and the door to the kitchen.

Something flitted by on the perimeter of light, on the path that led toward the barn.

Jennifer was stock-still, trembling. "Did you see it?" she whispered. "All in white like a——"

"Nonsense," said Rachel practically. "That was Mrs. Krythe."

# CHAPTER FIVE

"WELL," SAID Miss Jennifer, "if that's the sort of person she is—slipping and spying about at midnight and perhaps frightening people with dolls—I shouldn't encourage her acquaintance. And Miriam ought to know!"

"Perhaps Miriam does know. And saying that Mrs. Krythe performed the unpleasant trick with the doll is jumping to a conclusion; I didn't notice that she carried anything resembling a doll. There may be a perfectly normal reason for her being here, like looking for her needle."

"Rachel! That's fantastic!"

"Well, I don't expect people to behave always as I would, any more than that they should all like murder pictures."

"Movies!" cried Miss Jennifer, inhaling. "When I think of you and your purple horrors——"

"Because somebody must like musicals, even if the plots are always the same. Or those other pictures where for some strange silly reason the boy and girl have to share an apartment or a boat or a fire escape and of course——"

"Rachel!"

"Jumping again, Jennifer. Haven't you heard of Mr. Will

Hays? I was saying: And of course start by loathing each other and end by getting married. The trouble with the Victorian attitude——"

"By which you mean mine!"

"—is that it constantly confused life with fiction, to the detriment of the latter. I can't explain things to you any further just now, Jennifer. I want to go and see what Mrs. Krythe is doing."

"Spying on a spy!" choked Jennifer. "There's nothing worse."

"Go into the kitchen and make some tea. Take the cat with you. If you see Miriam you can tell her about Mrs. Krythe."

She hurried for the path that led to the barn while Jennifer delivered a few scorching bits concerning Miss Rachel's moral state.

The space behind the garages was a well of darkness, since the thin moonlight was cut off by the height of the barn and the trees. Miss Rachel felt her way, made out dimly the white fence of the corral, the shadowy outline of the big barn door. She stood quietly to listen. There was, through the open upper panel, a sound of crying and a low voice meant to comfort.

She was aware of a little qualm. The crying was Mrs. Krythe's. It was not ordinary sobbing, not the sort one listens to indifferently: it was deep, tearing, full of fury and despair. Miss Rachel felt a deep uneasiness, a prickling as though a battalion of needles had walked up her spine into her hair.

She wished suddenly that she hadn't followed Mrs. Krythe.

The answering voice was the voice of Checkers. She made out words: "You can't help him now. Don't give her the satisfaction of knowing how you feel. Remember Jerry, he's so young."

"So defenseless!" ground out Mrs. Krythe.

"He's not like Dave. We won't let him be. We'll warn him, teach him. There has to be a way he can hang onto some of it."

The sound of Mrs. Krythe's grief went on.

"When did you get the telegram?" asked Checkers.

"About noon. I—I've been sort of dazed. I haven't c-cried till now."

"You shouldn't have ever come here," Checkers worried. "You shouldn't have had anything more to do with her."

"She knows. . . ." Mrs. Krythe made a sound as though something had been torn out of her. "She knows she killed him."

"Sure she knows it. She wouldn't be fazed by it though. She'll make you an offer to clear the title. Don't take it."

"When Dave went away——"

"Don't talk about that," Checkers said gently. "Don't let your mind go back. Think about Jerry and the things you've got to do to protect his rights. Just settle yourself that it's all business from here out."

"How can I protect his rights?" Mrs. Krythe's voice shook and outside, in the dark, Miss Rachel sensed the fury and hatred that consumed her. "With my bare hands? With the truth about Dave? How far would I get with those?"

"Quiet now. Steady does it. We'll get hold of a good honest lawyer."

"To fight Braudryck?" She laughed breathlessly.

"Braudryck's just a man. He ain't a damned mind reader. How'll he know what you're going to do? Don't give him a hint either."

"I won't," Mrs. Krythe said after a pause. The suddenly quiet tone, the check on all emotion, reminded Miss Rachel of the appearance Mrs. Krythe had made on the terrace: drab, work-worn sub-subservient.

"Now that's better," said Checkers comfortingly. "You take

things as easy as you can. Stay away from here too. Maybe I could see you part way home."

"I know the way." Her tone was frozen and weary; Miss Rachel liked it even less than the bitter weeping. "I'll get along."

"I want to make sure you get down the hill all right," Checkers pondered. "You oughtn't to use the road. Braudryck's apt to rush down quick and quiet in that big car of his and see you. We wouldn't want any trouble, for Jerry's sake. There's too much depends on keeping everything to ourselves."

"I'll keep off the road," Mrs. Krythe told him. "Don't worry about me. You were always Dave's good friend and I know you're interested in Jerry, but I didn't have any right coming up here and maybe causing you to lose your job."

"I'm not afraid of that," Checkers said. "Look. I know my way down the grove pretty good; I guess I could manage coming back."

"No, don't take the chance."

"Wait a minute while I light my pipe." There was the scratch of a match. The interior of the barn was cavern-big, hollow with shadow in the brief, flickering yellow glow. "Shouldn't have done that," said Checkers. "Since I've got so blind I forget how other folks can see."

"I'm going. I'll see you soon."

The dark gave forth the stirrings of departure, the rattle of the hasp on the big door. Miss Rachel went away. She felt deeply disturbed by what she had overheard between these two people; their emotion had been genuine and their planning—on Checkers's part, at least—selfless; and she had, as Jennifer had truthfully put it, played the part of a spy.

She wondered how she might find out who Dave was and what had happened to him.

She found the kitchen door on the other side of Mr. Braudryck's big car and went in, rather subdued, to where Jennifer was pouring tea.

"No one's been here," said Miss Jennifer, "and I don't like it."

Miss Rachel looked at her meekly in question.

"There are too many people outside and too few inside. It's nearly one o'clock." Miss Rachel obediently studied the electric clock above Miriam's electric range. Miss Jennifer rattled a teacup suddenly in its saucer. "What became of Mrs. Krythe?"

"She's gone."

"Don't tell me you suppose she found her needle."

"Or perhaps Miriam's place is a short cut home."

"Up and down Miriam's hill?" Miss Jennifer put the china teapot down slowly; she had grown quite stern and there was a light in her eye. It was the light that usually appeared when she intended to tell Miss Rachel a few facts for her own good. They were invariably unpleasant facts. "Rachel, I'm beginning to smell a mouse."

"In here?" cried Rachel foolishly, looking about.

"Stop clowning." She made her mouth prim. "When you start telling falsehoods there's usually something upsetting on its way. Something gruesome. Like m—— No, I won't say the word. I refuse to believe that just because you've come, when everything has been peaceful and quiet——" She broke off. "Rachel, just why *did* you come to Miriam's?"

"I've told you."

"You said that you saw through the story about the water shares."

Miss Rachel studied the surface of her tea where the reflection of the light glimmered roundly. "Mr. Dewel was trying so hard and so nervously to put over the story that I thought it must be something he knew wasn't the truth."

"Then why, Rachel——"

Miss Rachel broke the reflection on the tea by moving the cup; the round light spattered and spread. "It seemed to me that the truth might be so much more interesting."

Miss Jennifer pounced. "There, Rachel, is your fault. You were eager, even avid, to get into the middle of this unpleasant business, whatever it is, like a frog in a pond, with your finger in everybody's pie and your nose at everybody's keyhole——"

"Quit scattering me about," Miss Rachel murmured, "and knit up a few of those metaphors." She stopped abruptly to listen. Muffled, popping, uneven, came the explosions of a motor.

Miss Jennifer listened with her eyes glued to the kitchen door. "Mr. Braudryck's car," she said.

Miss Rachel thought that the sputtering bark was more like that of Jerry Krythe's truck, but she forbore worrying Jennifer with it. The sound grew fainter gradually, at last died away.

Miss Jennifer cleared the tea things quickly. "Scolding you doesn't help. I should know better. I should remember the time you caught a moth and saved it to put in Cousin Zachary's beard. Nothing I could say——"

"The experiment with the moth would have gone on splendidly if Cousin Zachary had taken his after-dinner nap like an ordinary person. How was I to know that after he slept awhile his mouth always dropped open?"

"And he claimed that he had stomach flutterings for days——"

"I never believed that part of it. A cocoon, maybe. We were studying cocoons then in Miss Petterby's fourth grade. But not flying back and forth through the kind of meals Cousin Zachary could put away."

"But *anyway,* Rachel——" Miss Jennifer sagged a little. "I don't want to stay here, with people snooping about and someone trying to frighten Miriam by showing her a doll—I suppose they meant it for Miriam—and the story about the water shares just a fraud."

"We'll leave in the morning," Miss Rachel promised.

"And you won't have words with Miriam?"

"No. I'm tired and my anger's worn out. Miriam promised us a check. I'm going to take it and turn it over to the Red Cross."

"Should we tell her about the doll?"

"I rather think Miriam has seen it."

Miss Jennifer, drying the last teacup, dropped her voice to a whisper. "What could it *mean,* Rachel?"

"I'm trying to think," Miss Rachel said. "There's a twitch of familiarity about that doll somehow. I've seen it, or I've had it described to me. Not broken, not dirty; I don't mean looking the way it is now." She frowned, trying to dig an elusive memory out of her mind.

"If you remember in the middle of the night the way you do sometimes, come and wake me, will you?"

Miss Rachel promised and they went upstairs.

Jennifer, getting into her tentlike gown on the other side of the connecting bath, asked: "What do you think about Mr. Braudryck?"

For some reason Mr. Braudryck reminded Miss Rachel of a cartoon figure she had seen recently at a theater: a wolf wearing spats. But since Jennifer disapproved of her incessant movie-going, Miss Rachel saved her feelings by murmuring: "A smooth, professional kind of man."

"Do you suppose Miriam's lined him up? Matrimonially, I mean. The way she did Mr. Hamilton."

"It's possible."

"I didn't like his eyes," Miss Jennifer said surprisingly. "They laughed in a different way than his mouth did."

Miss Rachel, asleep at last, dreamed horrid dreams in which a wolf with spats chuckled gruesomely.

She was awakened by someone plucking at her and whispering. She thought that Jennifer might have grown nervous and come to sleep in the same bed. She moved over a little. The plucking and whispering went on.

Miss Rachel sat up and opened sleepy eyes and saw the windy gray skies of morning outside her window and, near at hand, the face of Miriam's maid. The girl was wearing a striped morning uniform, a frilled blue apron, and little cap. She was quite pale and she was trembling.

"Did you hear me, Miss Murdock?" asked the girl. "Mrs. Hamilton seems very queer. I'm afraid there's something wrong. Will you come and take a look and see what should be done?"

Miss Rachel sat quite still for a moment. There flashed through her mind the wavering and peering face of the doll, the ironic message to Joe Dewel, the wisteria seeds, the midnight visit of Mr. Braudryck: all scraps out of Miriam's basket of intrigue and ruthless purpose, straws blowing before the winds of disaster. She looked again into the face of the maid, waxy and shaking, and she had a sudden hunch that Miriam's troubles had caught up with her.

"I'll come at once," she said. She scrambled into slippers, threw the robe over her gown and knotted its belt, and followed the maid out of the room. The air of the hall was faintly chilly, faintly smelling of the oiled machinery of the air-conditioning unit in the roof. The light above the stairs, still burning in daylight, gave an odd look of dissipation to the scene.

The cat had followed like a shadow. Now at the door to Miriam's room she paused and a ridge of black hairs grew up along her spine.

The maid reached ahead to push open the door and they went in.

Miriam Hamilton had never really been beautiful. She had had a dark, imperious, delicately boned face; black hair of a peculiar sooty softness; the long limbs and the graceful carriage of an aristocrat. She had had unusual hands: narrow, agile, expressive. Making the most of what she had, wisely and expensively, she had emerged from the ministrations of her beautician, her dressmaker, and her maids as the picture of a great lady, chic and assured, in whom prettiness would have been a little common.

Nor was she pretty now. She lay among pillows, propped up somewhat, wearing a white chiffon negligee and a white crepe gown. A bed jacket of yellow angora wool had been pulled across her shoulders. Her dark hair was loose, shaken out across the pillows. Her half-closed eyes, fringed with mascara and eye shadow, were withdrawn and meditative. From the corner of her heavily rouged lips had run a tiny trickle of blood.

"Can we revive her?" whispered the maid.

Miss Rachel shook her head. Miriam Hamilton was coldly and completely and unmistakably dead.

# CHAPTER SIX

The maid's voice sounded as though it had come up from the bottom of a barrel. "Should I call Dr. Page, Miss Murdock?"

Miriam was obviously beyond the help of any doctor in this world. Touching her cold wrist, Miss Rachel found no stir of pulse. Her eyes were fixed, the eyelids grown ashy in color. The room itself was queerly deathlike. There was a hushed, enclosed feeling as though all movement had long ceased here; and the harsh gray light shone on the white linen, the smooth spread, the broad walls as inappropriately as into a tomb.

"Yes," answered Miss Rachel, "you had better call her physician."

The maid went away quickly and Miss Rachel remained.

The bank of windows across the room showed the tips of viny growth on the arbor and the gray opalescent sky. There were neither shades nor venetian blinds at the panes, but for drapery there was an immense panel of pale blue velvet embossed with a design in silver thread, and this was drawn aside. The light permeated the silent room and shone upon the figure in the bed.

Beside the bed stood a small table of blond wood; on it was placed a silver tray, a silver thermos jug etched with Miriam's monogram, two silver-rimmed glasses turned upside down, a bottle of aspirin, and beside the tray a hairbrush with an amber-colored mounting.

On the lace spread that covered the bed, just beside the rise of Miriam's knee, lay a matching comb and mirror, also amber-colored, and a bottle of mimosa cologne.

Miss Rachel, conscious of a feeling of depression and chill, drew away and walked to the windows. To the right she saw the edge of the terrace and the cypress thicket; nearer and below were the timbers of the framework which supported the honeysuckle, the neglected tangle of ferns and amaryllis, the path to the kitchen entry. Below, like the beginnings of a green sea, was the edge of Miriam's groves.

She turned to find the maid standing in the door. "I called the doctor, Miss Murdock. He's coming over."

Miss Rachel had seen the ivory phone and its cradle in the niche near Miriam's bed. She indicated it with a nod. "Why did you go out to telephone?"

"That is Mrs. Hamilton's private phone, miss." She stopped to look distraught. "Could we do something for her while he's coming?"

"There is nothing we can do," Miss Rachel told her. "Mrs. Hamilton is dead."

"Should I cover her with something then?"

"No, don't touch her at all."

The maid drew a little white handkerchief from the pocket of the ruffled apron and began to sniffle and to dab at her eyes.

"Stop that," said Miss Rachel. "I want to talk to you. When did you last see Mrs. Hamilton alive?"

The maid grew somewhat round-eyed, a little reproving, but

she put the handkerchief away. "I met her in the hall at about ten-thirty last night."

"Did you talk to her?"

"She asked me if anyone was up. I told her that you and your sister and Miss Hamilton and Mr. Flanders had just broken up your bridge game and gone to bed. She told me I might as well turn in for the night, too, that there wouldn't be anything she'd want me for. I might add, miss, that she was dressed for going out."

"Do you remember the clothes she wore?"

"She wore a green flannel suit and a black Persian lamb jacket. It was an outfit she was very fond of for informal wear, miss." The maid's eyes lengthened like a cat's as she looked sidewise at the bed. "I can't hardly stand here talking about her. I feel as if she's watching me."

"Did she say anything about Mr. Braudryck's coming?"

"Oh no, miss. Nothing."

"What did you do after talking to her?"

"I went right to bed."

"Who had the duty, incidentally, of turning down Mrs. Hamilton's bed and laying out her gown?"

"Well, I should have. I was Mrs. Hamilton's personal maid."

"And you had done this, then, previously?"

The maid shook her head; there was a look of evasion on her face, as though something in this line of questioning displeased her. "No, Miss Murdock. Ordinarily I should have. But lately . . . she had made a different arrangement."

Miss Rachel was studying the wide bed in its alcove. The lace spread was contrived with an intricate and feathery stitch, done by hand, new, and as soft as a cobweb. Miss Rachel estimated its worth, remembered Miriam's care with things that cost money. "Shouldn't her spread have been removed and some other cover put in its place for the night?"

The maid nodded, still with an air of unwillingness. "One of her puffy comforters, those taffeta things with goose feathers in them."

"And Mrs. Hamilton had been in the habit of doing this for herself?"

The maid must have read the unbelief in Miss Rachel's usually serene face. "I—well, I wasn't supposed to tell anyone. I oughtn't now, either, I guess, with her . . . Mrs. Hamilton's orders were strict."

"Go on," said Miss Rachel.

She swallowed, made a pleat in the apron with a nervous hand. "She told me a month or so ago I wasn't to come in this room any more after dark. Not for any excuse, I wasn't."

"Did she give you a reason?"

The maid grew round-eyed again. "Miss Murdock, I'm a maid. I don't ask my employers for reasons."

"Most of them do nowadays," said Miss Rachel. "But go on: didn't you wonder about not being allowed in here after nightfall?"

"No, miss," said the maid demurely, obviously lying.

Miss Rachel spent a few minutes studying the room. "Do you notice anything here that seems out of place or unusual?"

The maid looked about, avoiding the direction of the bed. "No, miss. Outside of the spread being left, I guess not."

"Was Mrs. Hamilton in the habit of brushing her hair at night?"

"I wouldn't know, miss."

Miss Rachel went on fishing. "And the aspirin on the table—was that supposed to be there?"

The maid took a sidelong look and shuddered. "I never knew Mrs. Hamilton to take aspirin or any drug, miss. But that wouldn't mean she hadn't started."

Miss Rachel asked, as if thoughtlessly: "How do you suppose she came to die like this?"

It popped out, the answer the maid must have instantly regretted: "Scared to death, I shouldn't wonder!"

"Oh." Miss Rachel's eyes seemed to be, like her mind, on other things. "Why do you say that?"

The maid wriggled. There must have been mental, secret wrigglings, too, over that chance remark. "Oh, I don't know. She seemed nervous recently."

"But you hadn't ever been in the room after dark, disobeying," said Miss Rachel, "the instructions Mrs. Hamilton had given. You hadn't seen that thing creeping up to the window."

The maid went through a spasm of denial, voicelessly: her hands rose and she shook her head and Miss Rachel could all but hear her knees knocking. Then she fled as though horror snapped at her heels, and Miss Rachel was alone.

Miss Rachel went to the closet, opening a mirrored panel that slid back into the wall. Miriam's clothes, enough to furnish a small shop, hung on a long rack. Miss Rachel, investigating, found that the rack could be swung round and pulled out into the room.

There was a whole section of suits: gray, fuchsia, navy, rust, green, white. There were, too, some dozen fur wraps of all sorts. Among them was a black Persian lamb jacket which seemed to fit the description given by the maid.

Miss Rachel suddenly didn't like the feeling in that room. She decided to go back to Jennifer.

She closed the door to Miriam's room and hurried along the halls. She found that Miss Jennifer had made a burrow out of her bedclothes and was crouched in them like a mouse in a cornshock. "The maid came in a moment ago and shrieked something at me," said Jennifer. "I think she's gone insane. Or else . . . something's very wrong."

"Miriam is dead," said Miss Rachel soberly.

Miss Jennifer drew several quite audible breaths. "Dead? In her room?"

"That's right: I think you'd better get up at once, Jennifer. If we go to the kitchen right away and have a bite of breakfast we'll be ready when things start happening later."

Miss Jennifer squeezed her eyes shut as though the sight of Rachel were strange and frightening. "How can you, Rachel? How can you casually toss off a death—a death in the family, at that—with a thought about hurrying down for breakfast?"

"Because," said Miss Rachel practically, "if we don't get breakfast right away we're apt not to have any. I have a feeling that when the police arrive they'll gather the cook up with the rest of the servants and keep them together with an officer on hand to listen to what they say while they're waiting to be interviewed. And meanwhile, being empty, we'll get that all-gone feeling—which the police, not being as acute always as they should, might take for a guilty weakness."

"Why do you keep harping on the police?" cried Jennifer.

"Even to my unofficial eye there were a few very queer things about Miriam's death. Now come and put on your clothes and we'll ask the cook for some coffee."

Miss Jennifer's nose twitched indignantly. "You always were

unfeeling, bold as brass, and disrespectful. Like the time when you were twelve and you embarrassed Aunt Sophie by tying her ruffled bust improver to her horse's tail."

"The street was full of flies and Aunt Sophie's horse wasn't," defended Miss Rachel with an air of being on old ground. "And anyway, she shouldn't have left him so long in the sun nor trimmed his tail just because it was fashionable."

"But an intimate garment like——"

"The bust ruffles did more for the horse than they did for Aunt Sophie," concluded Miss Rachel firmly. "They frightened the flies. On Aunt Sophie they were simply stuffy. Now do get up."

Miss Jennifer vanished except for the tip of her nose. "What caused Miriam to die, Rachel?"

A disturbed look came into Miss Rachel's eye. "I don't know. I wish I did."

"Poison?"

Miss Rachel was silent, remembering the grim figure on the bed.

Snappishly Miss Jennifer got out: "Aren't you troubled by any grief at all?"

"Somewhat, yes." Miss Rachel seemed to turn an introspective look upon her own emotions. "I think the grief I feel though, is for the little girl Miriam used to be, the wild black-haired child who loved dogs and horses and the out of doors and who hadn't learned yet to think so much of money. The rest is regret because Miriam got so little out of all she had."

"She got Ray Hamilton for a while. Wasn't it queer she couldn't keep him?" Miss Jennifer wriggled nervously inside the covers. "I don't suppose we can go home."

"I don't suppose we can. Do get up, Jennifer."

By dint of a great deal of coaxing she got Jennifer dressed

and down to the kitchen. A flustered and bumbling cook spilled coffee into two cups for them, made overdone toast, tried to find out the grimmer details about Miriam. They were eating at a chromelegged table in the corner of the kitchen when Sharon came in.

She must have dressed in haste; she was wearing the same black dress she had worn before but she had neglected to fasten it at the throat. Her skin was white and her eyes shadowy and enormous. She wore much the same expression she would have if someone had just dealt her a stinging slap in the face. She saw Miss Rachel. "It isn't true! Say that it isn't!"

"About Miriam?" asked Miss Rachel, trying to put calmness in her voice. "Yes, it is unfortunately true." She caught the attention of the gaping cook and nodded toward the coffee. "Sharon, you'd better have something hot with us."

Sharon advanced as if blindly. "But . . . *Miriam!*"

Miss Rachel pulled out a chair and Sharon stumbled into it. The silky brown hair fell across her eyes and she brushed it away mechanically. "Miriam was always so alive and so—so terribly sure of herself."

Mentally Miss Rachel agreed. Miriam had been sure enough of herself to be only temporarily worried by whatever evil was represented by the phantom doll, the mischief with the fuchsias. Perhaps Braudryck had his place in that assurance. Perhaps Miriam meant to see things through alone.

Sharon went on: "It's incredible that she should be dead. Even if she were hated the way I sometimes thought she was . . ." Sharon sat and looked into the cup the cook had put down for her. ". . . by the people who had grievances against her . . ."

She put her head down suddenly into her hands. A muffled

sound like Rick's name came through her fingers. Miss Rachel's little hand crept over to touch Sharon's firmly.

"Was she murdered?" Sharon said hoarsely.

"We don't know."

Miss Jennifer said with sudden kindness: "Don't weep so, child. Miriam wasn't the sort who'd want weeping done about her."

The maid came in then to say that Dr. Page had arrived and had been taken upstairs to Miriam's room. Miss Rachel saw that Sharon had no knowledge of what should be done. She went up to interview Dr. Page herself.

In the upper hall, just shutting the door of Miriam's room, was a small brown-faced man in a tweed overcoat.

He listened while Miss Rachel introduced herself. He had a sparse, gray-speckled mustache, direct eyes in which shone amazement and something like fear. He coughed before he spoke. "Mrs. Hamilton is dead. I think that I should use the telephone. I might explain that I intend to call the police."

Miss Rachel looked at him composedly. "Do you mean that Mrs. Hamilton was murdered?"

"I can't say in just what manner she met death." His voice cracked a little and he corrected it by lowering his tone to a more professional level. "Such matters are for the police. My findings are such that I cannot issue a death certificate, and in such case I must notify the coroner and official routine must take its course." He blinked and his brown eyes went beyond her to the maid. "A telephone, please."

"There is one in Mrs. Hamilton's room," said Miss Rachel.

"It is out of order," said Dr. Page stiffly.

He went away with the maid.

Miss Rachel opened the door of Miriam's room. The body of the dead woman had been moved slightly and lay straightened, covered by a sheet. The doctor's bag, unopened, sat on the blond wood table beside the silver thermos jug.

Something in the brief examination that Dr. Page had made had flushed him from his professional calm like a hare from a thicket. Miss Rachel wondered what it was.

# CHAPTER SEVEN

THE ARRIVAL of the police was prompt and businesslike. They came in like well-trained bloodhounds at the heels of the sheriff, whose name was Butterworth. A couple of highway patrolmen seemed to have tagged along out of curiosity. The house began to bustle with work, to resound to footsteps and voices.

Butterworth was a tall man with massive shoulders and a pose to his head as though he were listening to something he didn't believe. He had clipped dark hair, bright gray eyes, and a grim mouth. He dressed nothing like the motion picture sheriffs Miss Rachel had watched through innumerable movies, but wore a plain brown business suit, a brown snap-brim felt, a dark overcoat, and a maroon muffler. He knew Dr. Page and Sharon and Rick and spoke to them in greeting; the two Misses Murdock he seemed to regard with suspicion.

Dr. Page, while waiting for the arrival of someone official to take over, had assumed the task of rounding everybody up. The four maids and the cook and the laundress he settled in the kitchen. He found Checkers and another gardener in the grounds and brought them inside. He thought Mrs. Hamilton should have a chauffeur, too, but Checkers told him that Mrs.

Hamilton had enjoyed driving her cars. He might have added that after Ray Hamilton left her to go to France Miriam's always swift driving had taken on a quality of savagery and recklessness; but he didn't. Dr. Page went away to gather up the family.

He put Miss Rachel and Miss Jennifer and Sharon in Miriam's living room, bringing in Rick afterward. Across what seemed acres of lilac-colored broadloom carpeting, past furniture upholstered fatly in yellow velvet and corded at all the edges with pale blue, Miss Rachel watched the arrival, in the hall, of Butterworth and his men.

Miriam's great living room was a cavern done in pastels. Two white butterfly grands sat flank to flank in front of the main window, a ceiling-to-floor affair, which looked out at Miriam's valley. The lilac sponge underfoot was interrupted here and there by groups of furnishings, clustered with the intention of being cozy and looking instead somewhat lost. The bigness, the pale coloring, the unechoing silence, and the misty light gave the effect this morning of a sea charm, of a glimmering underwater dream. Miss Rachel, absent and distracted, wondered whether a mermaid might not swim up to look in at the window.

At about this time Mr. Butterworth, no figure of a mermaid and far too grimly intelligent for a fish, put his head in at the door. He spoke to Rick and Sharon, gave the Misses Murdock a look which implied that nothing like this had happened in his district until they arrived in it, and took Dr. Page upstairs.

Dr. Page was, it seemed, among other things, deputy coroner.

Butterworth came back presently, looking grimmer than ever. He settled himself in a yellow velvet chair and put his snap-brim felt on the floor. He looked at Sharon and Rick and the Misses Murdock for a moment in silence. "Mrs. Hamilton is dead," he said. "Of course you know that."

"I didn't," said Rick. He looked Butterworth in the eye. Miss Rachel got the impression there was no love lost between the two.

She remembered, too, with amazement that neither she nor Jennifer nor Sharon had said anything to Rick about Miriam; they had presumed that Dr. Page would have told him before bringing him to join the group.

"How come you didn't know it?" said Butterworth.

Rick had paled a little from the unexpected shock. "Nobody told me. Dr. Page came out and called, and said that I was wanted here in the living room. I supposed from his tone that there had been some sort of trouble, but I didn't think of death. I thought that perhaps Miriam meant to accuse somebody of something and wanted witnesses. That's the way she liked to handle things."

Butterworth's grim face lit up with interest. "Yeah? Just why did you have that idea?"

Rick frowned. "Miriam has been gunning for somebody lately. I knew her well enough to read the signs."

"Who?"

"I don't know."

Butterworth turned to Sharon. "Perhaps your sister knows then."

A peculiar expression came into Rick's face. His mouth tightened so suddenly that two paler patches sprang into being at the corners of his lips. He began abruptly to light a cigarette. "Sharon isn't my sister," he said quietly. "Remember?"

"Well, anyway . . ." said Butterworth; and he took a moment to squeeze the implications out of what Rick had just said. Miss Rachel sensed the wheels going round and the answer Butterworth was getting. But there wouldn't be anything strange about Rick's and Sharon's being in love, if they were, she thought: they were normal and likable young people. Having Miriam mutually for a stepmother didn't imply any relationship.

"Do you know, Miss Hamilton, whether your stepmother was after anyone, and for what reason?" Butterworth asked finally.

Sharon looked briefly at Miss Rachel. "She was worried about some mischief which had been going on. Some of her prize fuchsias had been ruined. I don't know whom she suspected." A spot of color came into Sharon's cheeks; she must be remembering that she had told Miss Rachel that Miriam suspected her. But Miss Rachel felt no criticism for the lie; Butterworth's grim truculence invited lying. She remembered her friend of the Los Angeles police, Lieutenant Mayhew, and his innocent quiet in talking with suspects.

"Fuchsias ruined?" said Butterworth. "That's a queer kind of thing."

"Miriam was very fond of her prize winners," Sharon explained. "That would be one very good way of rousing her anger." She drew a deep, slightly uneven breath. "You might ask Checkers, the gardener. He can explain better than I about the flowers."

Butterworth dug from the pocket of his overcoat a stiff-backed little notebook and a pencil with a frayed eraser. "I'll make a note of that. While I'm at it, any of you that knows something about Mrs. Hamilton's death might tell me now."

He looked at them expectantly as though one of them were going to tell him immediately how Miriam had died.

"What was the cause of death?" Rick asked.

Butterworth chewed the eraser a moment and looked at the floor. "We haven't found the weapon yet," he said.

He got out of them at last, and piecemeal, the story of the evening. He made notes about the Dewel brothers' departure after dinner, the bridge game between Sharon and Rick and Miss Jennifer and Miss Rachel, the game's breaking up a little after ten. Sharon told him that she had gone to her room immediately, to read awhile in bed and to turn off her light at about eleven-thirty. Rick had gone out to check the flow of irrigation water in the groves below the driveway. He had been there again when Dr. Page had called him this morning. He hadn't seen Miriam since yesterday morning when he had met her in the hall and she had greeted him absently and hadn't stopped to talk.

Sharon had last seen Miriam when she had taken Mrs. Krythe to the sunroom. Miriam had been there. Sharon had left the two women together talking about slip covers. It would have been, she thought, sometime between two and three yesterday afternoon.

Butterworth wrote Mrs. Krythe's name down in block capitals. Something about Mrs. Krythe's being here seemed to have given him a good deal of satisfaction.

Miss Rachel had begun meanwhile to feel queerly stifled. She had the sudden hunch that Butterworth wasn't going to believe the story about the doll. He had openly doubted the tricks with the fuchsias. The bobbing doll at Miriam's window was too fantastic, too subtle in its implication of horrors to come, for Butterworth's type of imagination to grasp. In his literal mind the story would be set down to an old lady's overactive imagination or to a desire to cloud the issue with a fairy tale.

He was ready for her and Jennifer now. He flicked over a new leaf in the notebook and gave them each a suspicious stare. Miss Rachel tried to wigwag Jennifer with her left eyebrow but Jennifer was watching Butterworth.

"Now, you ladies, please," said Butterworth. "Names, please."

They gave them.

"When did you last see Mrs. Hamilton?"

"We didn't," Miss Rachel said before Jennifer could get started. "You see, we came up from Los Angeles at her request yesterday afternoon. There were some business matters we were to discuss with Miriam. She didn't meet us nor did she come down to dinner. In fact I rather thought she avoided us during the evening." Miss Rachel frowned over the memory of Miriam's odd behavior. "Though I didn't see her, I talked with her."

"Oh," said Butterworth a little more happily. "When was this?"

"At about midnight. Miriam called me on the house telephone. We discussed our business affairs briefly. After I had hung up I talked with Jennifer and we thought it might be better if we saw Miriam personally."

"These business affairs," said Butterworth uneasily, as though he thought Miss Rachel were putting something over on him. "You might explain them a bit."

She gave him Joe Dewel's feeble story about the water shares and the gist of Miriam's conversation later over the house telephone. "So you see, the reason Miriam brought us here may have been the one Rick mentioned—she may have been after someone. In fact she must have been. Miriam wouldn't have taken the damage to her fuchsias lying down."

Butterworth looked at Rick as though Rick and Miss Rachel were trying to trick him. "And just why should she have brought you into this?" he asked, turning back to her.

This was the part which was going to be difficult. Butterworth would not love her, she knew, if he found out that she considered herself (and was considered highly by others) as an amateur detective.

"I'm a very old friend of Miriam's," she said innocently. "I suppose she thought two heads were better than one."

There is nothing like a platitude to soothe a policeman, she thought as Butterworth relaxed a trifle. "All right," he said, "let's go back to last night. You were setting out to find Mrs. Hamilton."

"We didn't find her in her room." She paused significantly; if Jennifer burst out with the shudders she could put in the part about the doll. But Jennifer was trying surreptitiously to read what Butterworth had written in his little book. "We went down finally to the terrace. There we came across Mr. Braudryck, her attorney."

"Ah," said Butterworth, "at midnight?"

"At midnight," said Miss Rachel, wondering how she might make Mr. Braudryck sound a little more suspicious. "Mr. Braudryck said that he and Miriam had been talking together on the terrace and that she had just gone in to bring out something hot to drink."

Butterworth seemed to reflect, to resist her suspicion of Mr. Braudryck as a goose might resist stuffing. But he asked: "Did you see any sign that she had been there? A coat, maybe, or something?"

He was quick, she admitted to herself. And this was something she hadn't thought of. She fed a little doubt into her voice. "No, I'm afraid there wasn't anything there of Miriam's. We had Mr. Braudryck's statement that she had been there though. Of course, not wishing to interrupt their private conversation, we left the terrace shortly."

"Wait a minute," Butterworth interrupted. "Didn't you just say that you were looking for Mrs. Hamilton so that *you* could talk to her? Why didn't you just wait on the terrace until she returned?"

His grim eyes waited for her answer. "Well . . . you see . . ."

She tried to think of something which might have kept them outside, taken them around to the back.

Miss Jennifer now looked up calmly, catching the narrative by its tail. "Oh, we were really looking for Miriam's window by then."

"Window?" Butterworth chewed his eraser gingerly. "I don't get it. Why?"

"We wanted to see it from outside," said Jennifer seriously. She hadn't been listening, then, when the part was omitted about the doll. Miss Rachel made wigwags with both eyebrows but Jennifer didn't see them. In her morning dress of dull gray voile, white hair skull-tight and skin grimly shining, Miss Jennifer looked like the female version of a gnome. If she'd just use one touch of powder, Miss Rachel thought disconnectedly, a bit of pink on her prim cheeks . . . "We wanted to see if there was any way that a person could get up to the window from out of doors," Jennifer said. "I mean, Rachel did. What I really wanted to do was to jump into bed and pull the bedclothes over my head until daylight. But Rachel isn't frightened so easily and I guess that part about the doll looking as though it had bled made her curious."

She must have seen how dead still and breathless they all sat. Rick had let his cigarette go out; his lean face was set in a curious expression, half disbelief, half trying to remember. Sharon was crouched small, still as a mouse inside the dull black dress.

"Dolls don't bleed, do they?" Miss Jennifer asked Butterworth.

A chunk of Butterworth's eraser disappeared between his teeth. "Huh? Wait. Begin all over again, won't you? Where did you find this thing, this doll or whatever it was that was bleeding?"

"Had bled," corrected Jennifer. "It came and goggled at us through Miriam's window. Rachel told you."

Butterworth threw Miss Rachel a look. "She didn't tell me. You tell me."

"I—it was so fantastic, I hardly thought you'd believe it," said Miss Rachel in a small voice.

She saw that Jennifer's staggering nonchalance had put over what no amount of emphasis could have; Butterworth was swallowing the doll story as eagerly as he had swallowed the bit of eraser. Perhaps he thought that Miss Rachel had tried to keep it from him.

Miss Jennifer told the story to Butterworth and he wrote it down. He tried then to get Rick or Sharon to say they'd seen the thing or knew what it meant. Rick answered uneasily that there was something about a doll that he was trying to remember.

Miss Rachel offered the information that the maid might have seen it since Miriam had ordered her to stay out of the room after dark.

Under Butterworth's insistence Sharon shook her head. She held her hands clenched together in her lap; Miss Rachel suspected that inside Sharon was as taut as a steel-wire fiddle string. She had grown even paler, a transparent dead-white color that was frightening. A pulse trembled unevenly under the smooth line of her jaw.

It came over Miss Rachel suddenly: the hunch that Sharon was lying. Sharon knew what the doll was. She knew what it meant.

# CHAPTER EIGHT

Miss Rachel sat on the edge of Jennifer's bed and listened to Jennifer's moan about being involved in a murder case.

"Do you know," she said, "I don't think either Butterworth or Dr. Page is sure that it is murder. There's something about the case that has them stopped . . . perhaps the absence of a weapon. They're probably off somewhere now chewing over the story about the doll and that business with Miriam's prize-winning fuchsias."

Miss Jennifer, at the window, said, "I saw them walking out with Checkers. They took the path to the pool but I think they turned off and went to the barn."

"He'll be showing them the damage among the flowers," Miss Rachel decided. Into her mind's eye rose the lath work, the creeping tangle of lantana and moon vine at the back of the barn. A sudden conviction came to her that she was missing a perfectly wonderful opportunity. She got off the bed and into a woolen jacket. The morning outside was still gray, inclined to fogginess almost as damp as rain.

"Where are you going?" asked Jennifer suspiciously.

"Walking," said Miss Rachel with innocence.

Jennifer wasn't fooled. "If Butterworth and Page catch you spying you'll hear some very unpleasant things about yourself. They'll be true too." Miss Jennifer rapped waspishly on the pane. "You aren't working with Lieutenant Mayhew now. Butterworth's a bear."

"You noticed it too?" Miss Rachel paused at the door. "If anyone asks for me I'm taking a bath."

"If they ask me where," Jennifer retorted, "I'll tell them you went off toward the pool with all of your clothes on."

"Don't do it, Jennifer; they'll merely think you queer." Miss Rachel went out into the hall. The sound of the sheriff's men was a murmur from the direction of Miriam's room. Miss Rachel peeped over the banister. In the hall below were two state policemen, looking at Miriam's collection of little pink marble nudes, each on a white pedestal like a rose on a milky stem. The state policemen, booted and harnessed, dressed in thick gray and leathered in the skin from being out of doors, had all the appearance of two interested bulls at the window of a china shop. Miss Rachel went down by the back stairs.

She crept past the garages light as a butterfly, on beside the high, heavily timbered walls of the barn, scooting low and like a shadow to keep beneath the level of the benches in the lath house. She could hear Butterworth's official bellow, Dr. Page's answering remarks, Checkers's voice between them as dry as the rustle of a leaf.

In the dusty concealment of the lantana Miss Rachel tucked in her skirts and sat still to listen.

"I'm just asking you how much you know," Butterworth was saying. "I'm not trying to pin anything on you. You can talk without putting yourself in wrong, can't you?"

"He never wrote to me," Checkers said uncertainly. "Whatever I heard of him, I heard it from her."

Miss Rachel tried to make sense of it, to connect it with the facts about Miriam.

"That was kind of queer, wasn't it? You and him used to be pretty good friends. I should of thought he could have dropped you a letter."

"He was pretty sick," said Dr. Page. "He might not have had the interest a normal man would."

"He was sick of all this valley," said Checkers. "Sick clear to the soul. I guess even sending a letter back here, except to his wife or Jerry, was more than he wanted to do."

The recollection of Checkers's talk last night with Mrs. Krythe came back: the talk that concerned someone named Dave, who had left something for Jerry Krythe that should be saved in spite of Braudryck's trickery.

"You might say, sort of, that Miriam Hamilton had a hand in what happened to Dave," said Butterworth slowly.

"You might," said Checkers. "Yes, I guess you might."

"Is that what Mrs. Krythe thinks?" Butterworth made this remark quickly.

"It is common knowledge that Mrs. Krythe thinks it," said Dr. Page. "Isn't that right, Checkers?"

Checkers must have missed the meaning of what he had said. "Dave wasn't no common man, Doctor. He was a right uncommon one, to my thinking. He had guts to get up on his hind legs and fight when Mrs. Hamilton and her lawyer went after his land. Dave Krythe was pure spunk, right down to his boots."

There was a little period of silence, as though the three men were remembering another, a man whose stout heart hadn't failed at the approach of Miriam's steam roller of wealth and power.

"Did you know," Butterworth asked after a pause, "that Mrs. Krythe was up here yesterday afternoon?"

"She must have known then," said Dr. Page musingly, "that her husband had died. The sanitarium would have notified her. I can't understand her coming here to do work for Mrs. Hamilton. Unless, of course. . ."

"Ummmn," said Butterworth. "Did you see her, Checkers?"

Checkers had had a moment to think over what he had to say. There was a fractional pause as though he drew a good breath to say it with. "No, I didn't see her. I didn't know she'd come."

*Wrong,* Miss Rachel told him voicelessly; *you could have said you'd seen her and that she wasn't bitter. You'd have been playing a shrewder game for Jerry in that way.*

"Well," said Butterworth abruptly, "let's see these flowers Mrs. Hamilton was so fond of." He sounded impatient, unimpressed, as though getting off the good solid motives of Mrs. Krythe and into the bog of mischief-making and malice was little to his taste. "Can't say that I see much sense to this. What would a woman as rich as Mrs. Hamilton care for the ruin of a few plants? Huh?"

Checkers made a painstaking explanation of Miriam's pride in her fuchsias, of how she garnered the prizes in the shows avidly, displayed them as a huntress shows her game. He didn't explain, as Miss Rachel knew, that Miriam had filled her life, after Ray Hamilton's going, with such stuff as came to hand and could in the bargain give her a sense of conquering.

They rattled pots inside the lath house and Butterworth made sour sounds at what Checkers showed him. Miss Rachel, meanwhile, looked behind her to find that her cat had followed and was playing busily with the dried undergrowth in the lantana.

"Shhh!" whispered Miss Rachel, reaching a cautious hand. The cat sprang away, stood sniffing at the laths.

"I guess that's all we'll need you for," Butterworth said at last. "You needn't mention any of this about the flowers, incidentally."

"Mrs. Hamilton told me that," said Checkers. He moved off with a crunch of boot soles on the gravel. There was silence on the part of the sheriff and Dr. Page until he had gone.

"Well, what do you think?" asked Butterworth.

"He took a while to answer the question about having seen Mrs. Krythe," said Dr. Page shrewdly.

"He didn't act rattled though. I didn't see any expression of fear on him."

"That may be accounted for by the fact that he's so near to being blind. He couldn't read our expressions, didn't answer with any of his own. What do you make of the fuchsia business?"

"Doesn't seem like much to me," said Butterworth. "Kind of kid stuff, petty mischief. Wait, I've just remembered something. Old lady Crane in the village accused Jerry Krythe of trampling her hedge when she wouldn't trim it."

"That doesn't sound much like Jerry," said Dr. Page.

"Well, Jerry claimed that the branches of the hedge were soiling his mother's laundry. The hedge divides the two back yards, see, and Mrs. Krythe's clothes didn't have room to hang, with the hedge the way it was. I got the old lady to trim her hedge and I gave Jerry a lecture. What I'm getting at is that the kid's very defensive about his mother."

"I guess he inherited some of Dave's spunk. I'd hate to see him mixed up in this affair, incidentally."

"Well," said Butterworth after a pause, "we know that he was up here yesterday in a car. That truck of his. It's not heavy but——"

"I haven't said that Mrs. Hamilton was run down by a car,"

Dr. Page put in stiffly. "I said she was crushed, that her ribs were broken and plunged inward and that she gave signs of having been subjected to a great deal of pressure. Her pelvis seems to be dislocated. There are other fractures: her upper right arm, for instance."

"You said that her condition reminded you of the fellow that got caught under Dick Binney's cement truck," Butterworth defended. "So naturally I figured she was run over by a car."

"If it were a car," said Dr. Page, seeming a little puzzled, "there should be other signs: tire marks, facial abrasions, dirt or gravel or grass or some indication of where she lay. I don't like this case, Butterworth. There's been some clever covering up, if it was murder. If it were an accident, why not come out with the truth?" He paused as if waiting for Butterworth's answer, then repeated: "I don't like it at all."

"As for the dirt or gravel," Butterworth put in, "that could have been gotten rid of along with the change of clothes. Couldn't it?"

"The coroner and I will do a microscopic examination of her skin," Dr. Page decided. "Then we'll know."

"Do you think she lived any time after this thing—whatever it was—hit her?"

"Perhaps a few minutes. She'd be quite helpless, of course, and unable to make any sounds vocally."

"They might have carried her in still alive, then, and fixed her in the bed?"

"Yes, that's possible."

"I don't like it either," Butterworth said. "No sir. I don't like it one bit."

There were indications that the men were leaving the lath house. Miss Rachel crouched low. The bushes shook a little above her head. Then she realized, as coldly and certainly as though someone had spoken in the gray silence, that she was not alone in the tangle of viny growth, that another had listened as she had, crouched and watchful. She remembered the cat's antics and her nervousness. She turned slowly to peer through the jungle thicket full of bloom.

Mr. Joe Dewel was getting up from behind the lantana at the opposite edge of the barn. He didn't see Miss Rachel. He looked warily at the encroaching trees, into the lath house, and toward the front of the barn. Miss Rachel, frozen like a mouse which sees the inside of a cat's mouth closing toothily over it, felt that if he looked at her she should faint.

He was much more gray now than reddish. The melted-wax Santa Claus had been left out in the fog to fade, to frost with a clammy sweat. He wiped moisture from his brow, shook off the clinging dried bits of lantana leaves, then took a brown half-pint bottle from his hip pocket. He measured the liquid against the light, not cautiously as a habitual drinker portioning his whisky, but as though the absent and casual action gave him a moment in which to think.

When he was through with the bottle he tossed it away in the undergrowth and walked off through the trees, stumbling over clods as he went.

The cat, which had been as still as Miss Rachel herself, now crept over and with tail lightly fuzzed sniffed at the ground where he had passed.

Miss Rachel decided to leave there quickly. She called the cat, picked her up, walked back by way of the pool to the terrace. She saw, while she was still some distance from the railing, Sharon come out of the house carrying her typewriter and some paper. The girl put the machine on the wrought-iron table, sat down in front of it, opened the case, and ran a single sheet into the machine. She turned, hearing Miss Rachel's steps. The gray light accented her pallor and the pinched expression about her mouth. She was wearing a heavy black coat over her black dress. She waited while Miss Rachel approached.

Miss Rachel had decided to get the story of Dave Krythe from someone; but she sensed that Sharon, faced with some problem of her own, might not enjoy such discussion. Rick might prove co-operative, might know more than Sharon too. She stopped by the table. "I'd like to find Rick. Do you know where he is?"

Sharon studied her obliquely, as though the question might have more meaning than Miss Rachel had put into it. "No," she said, "I don't know. I haven't seen him since our talk with Butterworth."

"Would he be trying to carry on as usual? Working perhaps?"

"I don't think so. But I don't know where he went."

Miss Rachel received the distinct impression that Sharon was waiting for her to go before touching the keys of the machine. The sheet in the typewriter was run through to almost half its length. Whatever Sharon meant to put on it must be brief. An envelope lay on the table beside the machine. Miss Rachel tried to think of a tactful way to phrase her next remarks.

"Think twice, my dear, about anything you put into a letter just now," she offered. "And when you've finished, go over it carefully and just to be safe—mail it in the incinerator."

Sharon jerked her fingers away from the keyboard. "I'm not such a fool, really. Nor still a child."

"No; but you're upset; you're not yourself. We're all very much on edge because of what happened to Miriam. I am; I'm sure Jennifer is. And I can't help recalling a time when I was young, when I woke up after a nightmare in which I had dreamed that a friend of mine had been peculiarly horrid. I got up from bed and wrote a dreadful letter, still half asleep and seething over the dream. In the morning I could scarcely believe that it was something I had written."

"This thing that happened to Miriam," said Sharon stiffly, "wasn't a dream."

"Its influence on what you write now, though, may surprise you afterward," Miss Rachel warned. She looked at the bent head, the face turned stubbornly from hers, the silky hair beginning to dampen with the fog. "Couldn't you tell me," Miss Rachel asked, "what it is that troubles you?"

For an instant Sharon looked at her, thoughtful and considering, as though she might answer. But it was then that Mr. Bart Dewel came out upon the terrace from the house. He was brisk and brilliant in a sage-green jacket, mustard slacks, a black silk neck scarf embroidered with a Chinese dragon in purple and red, gilded of claw and scale. His terrier's eyes lit up at seeing Sharon, cooled somewhat when they came to Miss Rachel. His glossy hair, sharp face, and well-balanced body all radiated purpose as he bore down on Sharon. Sharon hadn't moved.

"Dreadful about Miriam," he said into the palm of Sharon's hand. "Though there were signs of the storm from way back, weren't there? Threats . . . though none of us took them seriously. Miriam didn't." He kissed her fingers lingeringly.

"I don't know what you mean," Sharon stammered.

"There's nothing to understand." His eyes told her something. "One of the maids was screaming gibberish to Butterworth about a doll as I came through the hall. I'm sure he won't pay any attention to such nonsense."

There was a look on Sharon's face as though her heart had just stopped in her, as though she listened incredulously and in vain for its next beat. She hadn't drawn her hand from Bart Dewel's.

She watched now while his fingers crept up to close about her wrist.

The fog had begun suddenly to disperse; it ran smokelike before the wind and the valley showed signs of widening, the sky of being blue. Bart Dewel kept on holding Sharon's wrist. "I walked over," he said, ignoring Miss Rachel. "I knew you'd need comforting and I hurried. Poor little girl." He bent so that he saw into the depths of Sharon's eyes. He tapped the envelope with his free hand. "I'll bet you were writing me a note, weren't you?"

Sharon threw a ragged glance at the blank sheet in the typewriter. "Yes," she said. "I was writing you a note."

"And here I am, ready to help." There was some undercurrent of macabre humor here, Miss Rachel thought. His mouth twitched over the words and he continued to hold Sharon's hand as though testing her. "I'll do anything you wish me to do."

She seemed to rouse, to follow the line he meant her to take. "There are some papers of my father's that will need to be gone over in the light of Miriam's death," she said. "You might help me with them. They're in his little studio, the one we lived in before we came here."

He nodded agreeably. "When should we go? Now?"

He patted her wrist and let it drop. Miss Rachel could suddenly stand the expression in Sharon's face no longer. She put in casually: "But, Sharon, you haven't had breakfast."

"She can eat at my place," said Bart Dewel confidently. "I'd just made a pot of coffee and I'll scramble some eggs. Come on, Sharon."

"And you promised Mr. Butterworth you'd explain further about the slip covers," Miss Rachel lied glibly, ignoring him as he had her. "He'll be quite angry if you leave just now."

Sharon looked up at her expressionlessly. "I'd forgotten, Bart. I'll meet you later. Say at one o'clock, at the studio."

He didn't take being balked gracefully. A corrugated patch grew upon his forehead and his mouth turned sulky. But he said, "All right then. One o'clock." His look at Miss Rachel promised not to love her any more.

It was very quiet on the terrace when his footsteps had died away. Sharon sat looking at the typewriter as if mesmerized. Miss Rachel tried—and could not—find the words to say what she thought of Mr. Bart Dewel. She loathed him and was a little afraid of him, and the frightening new thing was that Sharon, who had been so fiercely remote, was strangely meek to him now.

Trees dripped faintly off in the groves. A blackbird scolded from the cypress thicket, suddenly, as if disturbed.

Sharon bent suddenly and touched the catch of her typewriter case, beside her chair. The lid gaped. Her fingers stayed as they were, touching the catch. She made no move to open the case further. She seemed to be staring at something under the empty lid, lost in a thought whose shadow lay in her eyes.

Miss Rachel, feeling dismissed, walked away into the house.

She wondered if the bird in the cypress had been disturbed by someone hidden and listening. Could Joe Dewel have circled the house and spied upon his brother and Sharon? And should she, perhaps, tell Rick about the rendezvous at one o'clock?

# CHAPTER NINE

Miss Rachel, still carrying her cat, peeped in at Miss Jennifer in the study. Miss Jennifer had gone back to making french knots; she snipped a thread in the distinct manner of thus curing it of some fault—over-curiosity, Miss Rachel's conscience suggested—and her eye on Miss Rachel's figure was not friendly.

"I'm cold," Miss Rachel chattered. "I think I'll have some tea."

"You deserve to be cold," said Miss Jennifer, "and tea won't help you. Nothing will, so long as you snoop about in the fog."

"I wasn't the only one snooping," Miss Rachel defended. "Mr. Dewel, the one who brought us up here, was doing it too."

Miss Jennifer restrained any curiosity she might have felt over Mr. Dewel's actions. "His brother practically trampled me in the hall. Something had made him quite angry. I caught your name, among other things, while he retrieved my embroidery hoops. I think," she concluded waspishly, "that Mr. Bart Dewel doesn't like you."

"I'm not going to worry over that. Do you want some tea?"

"Presently." Miss Jennifer wasn't letting down her armor of disapproval. "I'll join you in a few minutes. I'm trying to think."

"About what?" said Miss Rachel, showing interest.

"Nothing," snapped Miss Jennifer, taking the head off a perfectly good french knot. She looked at her little scissors in outrage. Miss Rachel discreetly closed the door before blame could attach itself to her and went away to the kitchen.

The kitchen, all chrome and white enamel and full of disappearing gadgets, had always reminded Miss Rachel of a factory. It had a grim, streamlined efficiency that made an automaton of a cook. The cook, now reverting to what she was meant to be, was simply a red-faced plump woman on the verge of quitting the job. She took in the bold telepathic stare of Miss Rachel's cat toward a bottle of milk and listlessly got out a saucer. She spilled the milk on the linoleum; for an instant there was the threat of tears and hysterics. Miss Rachel put on a kettle of water and then turned toward a window to give the cook time to compose herself. The window looked out at the foggy drive.

Mr. Braudryck's long car stood there, frosted with beady tracks of moisture as though a host of little spiders had walked over it with wet feet.

Miss Rachel's interest quickened. "Did you see Mr. Braudryck come in?"

"Yes," said the cook, mopping the milk. "He came through here a few minutes ago with the sheriff and Dr. Page. I think they met him in the drive. What should I do about lunch, Miss Murdock? Will we need to eat?"

"Definitely," said Miss Rachel. "We may have to serve Mr. Butterworth and Dr. Page too. Did Mr. Braudryck mention how long he meant to stay?"

"I wasn't listening," said the cook. She put away the mop and began to explore the refrigerator. "I was thinking how much I have to do and how little time to do it in." Plainly she was of a mind to forget meal planning and give way to shudders.

"I don't suppose they were talking about Dave Krythe," said Miss Rachel experimentally.

"Mr. Krythe? Why should they? Anyway, there's nothing but good to be said of him." She rattled glassware. "He's better than he's got, you mark it."

Miss Rachel looked at her thoughtfully. "I believe that Mr. Krythe is dead."

The cook's back straightened in its apron and her round eyes gave a cow look over her shoulder. "That's dreadful, though I'm not awfully surprised. He's been sick for ever so long. Bell Krythe says he overworked and strained himself on the land he was trying to clear. That was part of it, I guess." She brought out a dish of flaked crab meat and took it to the sink. Her eyes on the foggy window were regretful. "There was gossip for a while. Queer gossip for a woman Bell Krythe's age. I guess you know Checkers named one of his fuchsias after her. Would a soufflé and creamed crab do for lunch perhaps?"

"Very well indeed." Miss Rachel fixed the teapot and put boiling water into it, covering a feeling of sharp surprise. She summed up mentally the things she knew about Mrs. Krythe and Checkers: no story to suggest an illicit love, certainly. "I thought Mr. Krythe's troubles concerned an argument he had with Mrs. Hamilton."

"I'd heard that too," said the cook without interest, poking the crab meat with a fork.

Miss Rachel tried to fit the figure of Checkers, bent and gray and almost blind, into the role of a Don Juan. Humble and inarticulate people, she knew, had the romantic fancies of the most gifted; but there was some falseness, something basically out of character here. She couldn't quite pin the impression down. The Don Juan pattern left portions of Checkers sticking out around the edges. She poured her tea and sat down to drink it, full of busy thought.

Checkers had called his fuchsia Bonnie Bell, true enough. Bonnie Bell had been killed by a sharp cut above the roots. Miss Rachel recalled, almost unwillingly, the story of Jerry's damage to the neighbor's hedge.

In his talk with Mrs. Krythe in the barn Checkers had been all solicitude about Jerry's future. Was Jerry equally as fond of the old friend of his father's?

The cook having lapsed into gloomy silence and the intricacies of preparing a soufflé, Miss Rachel left the kitchen when her tea was gone. The memory of Sharon on the terrace sent her back there, but now everything was empty in the feeble sunlight. The fog had left a wet sheen on the metal table. A faint smoke rose off the bricks where the sun had begun to warm them and the groves below were full of the sound of dripping moisture. Miss Rachel stood quiet, listening, and felt an odd, prickling sense of danger steal over her. She remembered Sharon's engagement to meet Bart Dewel at her father's old studio, and her own impulse to tell Rick about it. Should she tell him, too, of Mr. Dewel's peculiarly unpleasant manner? She decided not to; there was so little of that which had disturbed her which she could put into words.

On the hunt now for Rick, she ran into Miss Jennifer in the hall. Miss Jennifer had her embroidery folded into a packet and her expression was belligerent. "You've had tea already?" she asked.

"Yes," said Miss Rachel, trying to be demure, "I've had it and it was quite refreshing. You should have some."

"I rather think you're up to some new trick," said Miss Jennifer suspiciously, "or you wouldn't be putting on this horrid pretense of thoughtfulness."

"I really am thoughtful," defended Miss Rachel. "I want you to enjoy your tea."

"And linger over it, and be a long while in the kitchen." Miss Jennifer's plain face took on a look of sarcasm which, in Miss Rachel's vivid imagination, made her look exactly like a hen. "When you were eight—and it should have made an impression on you—Father tied a red string to your finger for poking it into Aunt Rebecca's pompadour. And to remind you never to——"

"I'd always suspected it was socks," Miss Rachel put in dreamily. "There were bulges."

"What on earth," cried Jennifer, "are you talking about now?"

"The pompadour. Aunt Rebecca was too tight to buy a rat. She stuffed the pompadour with Uncle Steven's socks. The mended spots showed now and then too."

For a long moment Jennifer stood there and tried to think of something to say. Miss Rachel smoothed her skirt; for the fraction of a second the Victorian frosting cracked to show the merriment within. Miss Jennifer said bitterly: "I won't keep you, Rachel. I'll go and have my tea."

Miss Rachel put out a contrite hand but Jennifer swept by, breathing outrage. "If you see Rick," Miss Rachel said, "tell him to look in at the old Hamilton studio about one o'clock."

Miss Jennifer didn't answer.

The cat showed interest in Miss Jennifer's march toward the kitchen, hesitating at the tip of Miss Rachel's toe; but when Miss Rachel slipped out through the side entrance to the drive she found that her cat was with her. The two officers who had been admiring Miriam's collection of little statues were now supervising the arrival and parking of the ambulance from the morgue. To Miss Rachel's question as to where Rick might be, they answered that they hadn't seen him. The big gray ambulance drew up and Miss Rachel, having no desire to see what she knew would follow, walked away.

The thin new sunlight dappled the wet grasses of the corral, made the gloom inside the barn thick and cavernous. Hoping that Rick might be about, Miss Rachel stood in the doorway to listen. From somewhere off in the groves another blackbird scolded. She smelled the dry, cobwebby smell of the old barn, which must predate Miriam's mansion, and the raw odor of gasoline from the tractor. She picked her way past the litter of tools and looked across the closed lower half of the door to the lath house. The brilliant, jewellike colors of the fuchsias looked a little unreal in the gray light. The air that touched her cheek was cold with moisture. The memory of Bonnie Bell, of the damage that had seemed childish and pointless, set her tugging at the heavy hasp. The door moved sluggishly with a faint squeak of hinges. Some splinters at its edge touched her skirt, pulled at the fabric. She stood suddenly quiet, looking down.

There was a gash in the wood on the other side of the door, a deep raw mark with a curl to it like that of a whip, pale on a surface darkened by age. As Miss Rachel put an experimental finger on it splinters fell at her touch and the door, completing its arc, came to rest against the wall, fitting its upper half with a soft scrape of wood that made the silence afterward seem more intense. Miss Rachel's fascinated stare traveled from the scar upon the wood to the tractor, to a projection of its iron undercarriage where cultivating equipment could be attached. The heavy tires, the humped engine cast a shadow like some great squatting bug.

Miss Rachel felt as though everything were rushing together, fitting like links in a chain, and her mind turned unwillingly from the horror suggested by the mark on the door and the heavy machine. As if to convince herself that the thing couldn't be, she pulled the two sections of door outward and slid in behind them. By shrinking down a trifle, she had a fuzzy view of the barn through the crack between the sections. She saw the gray brightness at the big door, the gloom that seemed gathered in the corners, the shape of the tractor like something waiting and deadly.

"Now I'm going to think," she said half aloud to herself; and her own thoughts answered: You don't have to think. It's all here as though it had been written out for you. Miss Rachel shivered, knowing the truth and the terrible thing that had been done here.

From the courtyard outside, muffled by the wet grass, came the sound of walking. It was quiet walking, hollow against the silence laid down by the fog, and caution followed every step like an echo.

A shadow came to bisect the door, a wavering and uncertain shape in the narrow distortion of the crack. Miss Rachel sucked in a slow breath and swallowed hard. If it makes a move toward that tractor, she thought, I'm going to scream. Just a move. A step. Only, of course, if the person coming in hadn't meant any harm I'd look very foolish. . . . I'd better wait till I'm sure.

She realized with a mental brake skidding that this particular line of reasoning must have run through Miriam's head just before the monstrous end of everything, last night.

Steps came in cautiously upon the plank floor and Miss Rachel opened her mouth, getting ready.

Checkers's voice, painfully hesitant, said loudly: "Miss Murdock? Are you in here? Miss Sharon wants you."

The cat, utterly perfidious, meowed loudly from the door to the lath house.

"Miss Murdock?" He went past; his feet made scratchy noises in the wet gravel. "Miss Sharon would like to talk with you. She's out beside the pool."

Miss Rachel ducked out neatly and stole through the scattered tools and out into the corral. She scurried in the shadow of the garages, down a flagstone ramp overhung with ivy geraniums. She came to the pool, flat and silvery under the foggy light, and found the sun deck empty. Above she could see the corner of Miriam's house and a part of the terrace. There was no one in sight anywhere.

She looked about, expecting the black shape of Samantha, and found that missing also. A queer sense of desolateness, of being utterly alone, chilled her. She remembered wistfully the bright warmth of the kitchen where Miss Jennifer would now be having tea—not wistfully enough, though, to go back to it.

She recalled with uneasiness, too, Sharon's odd intentness over something inside her typewriter case; and the fact that Sharon, growing impatient, might even now have walked off to meet Bart Dewel.

Miss Rachel remembered vaguely in which direction Ray Hamilton's old studio lay. There once had been a path through the groves, she knew. Shortly before he had gone off to Europe Ray Hamilton had had the path cleared and surfaced with gravel. Something Miriam had said once, bitterly and in temper, had made Miss Rachel think that in the end Ray had lived there.

She left the wide cement sun deck beside the pool and explored the rock garden below it. At the bottom of some steps were three paths, none of which led in the direction she wanted. She hesitated, and the sounds that drifted to her out of the grove were muffled and echoing. From far off, from some other hill, came the rough sputter of a tractor motor. There had been the same sound last night, while she and Jennifer had been in the kitchen. She and Jennifer had heard it.

They had heard Miriam dying. She shuddered.

Miriam must have hidden behind the inner door of the barn. Perhaps she had hidden there to listen to Checkers and Mrs. Krythe. Perhaps she had fled there in the moments after they had gone, to hide from someone else—from whoever had raised that horrible doll to her window. She hadn't thought of the danger that waited for her in her hiding place. There must have been a moment of tinkering over the tractor which had puzzled her. Then the motor had coughed to life, the heavy wheels had gripped the floor, and Death had spun down on her like the falling of a mountain.

Miss Rachel rubbed her temples under the white line of her hair. Miriam had died in a way peculiarly horrible.

At the edge of the step something shifted under her shoe. She glanced down. On the surface of the stone was a little pile of sawdust, by it a ripped piece of cotton cloth.

She bent and picked up the piece of cloth. It was pinkish, close-woven, heavily glazed.

The color and texture reminded her of something she had known familiarly long ago. She turned it, smoothed it, trying to remember. The sawdust, too, fitted the teasing memory. The sawdust and the vaguely flesh-colored cloth . . . Of course. *A doll.*

The sawdust-stuffed body of a doll . . .

She hurried down the left-hand path at the head of which the scrap of cloth had lain. Deep in the grove, between two walls of greenery, the path turned in the direction she had remembered. She ran now, holding her skirts up in a manner Miss Jennifer would have thought scandalous, breathing hard, feeling her heart thump. She knew that now she made no picture of a Dresden lady. More likely she resembled a witch.

And, witchlike, she felt that the forces of evil thundered on ahead.

# CHAPTER TEN

THE PATH began to climb. There was a subtle change in the soil. The spaces between the trees grew larger and where the cultivator had passed were turned up stones and patches of sand. The rich loam that Miriam had coveted was gone.

The path came out between the trunks of eucalyptus forming a windbreak. Ahead was a hillside, planted with a few starved lemon trees in two small sections, the rest grown over with wild brush and manzanita. On the crest of the first rise sat the house Ray Hamilton had built for himself and Sharon. Miss Rachel had been in it once long ago. There was a foundation of rough stonework, then redwood timbers stained brown, a bank of cheap wavy-paned windows, and a roof of tile. The effect, in the midst of the uncleared brush, was rather pleasing. It was a man's house and an artist's house. It blended with its surroundings, it had been cheap to build, and there was no nonsense or frippery about it.

The path rose steeply toward it. Here and there the rise was divided by embankments and steps reinforced with desert stone.

Miss Rachel left the shadow of the eucalyptus. As she did so Sharon Hamilton came out of her father's house. She walked erratically, stumbling, and she seemed to be washing her hands. When she had finished rubbing her palms together she looked at them intently and then put them against her black skirt and rubbed hard.

There was something unaware, almost hypnotic, in her preoccupation with her hands.

"Sharon!" said Miss Rachel imperatively.

The girl paused. The blankness in her face didn't change but Miss Rachel saw the shivering start she gave.

"Sharon, wait!" Miss Rachel began to hurry, to cut down the distance between them. Sharon had stopped at the edge of the first embankment, peering down its slope as if into an abyss.

There were patches of dead grass, soaked now with moisture, which clung to the fringe of Miss Rachel's petticoat and slapped her ankles through her hose. The gray light, the silence, the look in Sharon's face sent a hollow fear through her. She forced herself to think of the hill and how it would change during the winter. In January it would begin to turn green. By next March it would bloom with wild flowers: poppies and lupine and those little wild blue lilies whose bulbs she and Jennifer ate and got sick on in that springtime long ago.

She had convinced Jennifer that the bulbs were edible, a fiction she had evolved along with the idea that they might become wild children and live off the country.

She thought of the seeds of poppy and lupine even now safely tucked into the ground, and the bulbs of the blue lilies waiting for spring. And the sense of floweriness, of beauty turned twisted and hideous, returned to haunt her.

Sharon's gaze seemed suddenly to narrow. She jumped down the embankment and caught Miss Rachel's arm.

"You mustn't go in the house." It was kindly. A kindly warning.

"Why can't I?" demanded Miss Rachel.

Sharon brushed as if at a cobweb. "Because you're a very nice little old lady. I've always liked you so much. Do come away."

"You've had a bad shock," Miss Rachel decided. "Now sit down on this bottom ledge while I go and see what's wrong."

She tried to make Sharon sit and Sharon tried to lead her down the path. They were each bent on taking care of the other. After some moments of this Miss Rachel lost her temper.

"Quit treating me as if I were *old*," she snapped. And then, as if this left something to argue over: "Or a ninny."

She went briskly up to the door of Ray Hamilton's studio and pushed it open. The room was very shabbily furnished. Some of the chairs were little more than benches, roughly put together out of left-over redwood. There were cushions of calico, faded now, that Sharon had made when she was very young. The bank of windows let in a lot of gray light. The long studio room was empty.

She glanced into each of the two narrow cubicles which were meant for bedrooms. There were cots here, and bare mattresses. Next was the bathroom, even smaller. She turned toward the door to the kitchen.

The kitchen was long. Near the door were stove and sink and a battered icebox with door swung open to show its empty, rusted compartments. At the other end was a big window and below it a breakfast table and two chairs.

Bart Dewel was sitting at the table. His head was resting on his arms as though he were sleeping. In front of him was a bottle of brandy, about half full, and a couple of glasses.

There was a step behind Miss Rachel and she looked back. Sharon plucked at her arm. "Come away! *Don't look at him!*"

There was an oddly shaped projection above the brilliant collar of Bart Dewel's jacket. For an instant Miss Rachel thought that he might have put his right arm all the way under and around and that one of his fingers pointed upward on that other side. Then she saw that the flesh-colored object more resembled something else: a miniature hand.

She went closer and Sharon's shuddering words followed, begging. The miniature hand and wrist stuck out of the base of Bart Dewel's skull.

There was a terrible stillness about the way he sat, crouched forward. Miss Rachel swallowed her terror and put out her fingers to touch the skin of his exposed neck.

"Don't!" Sharon screamed. Then, sobbing: "He's dead . . . dead."

He was indeed dead.

A dreadful, impelling curiosity took Miss Rachel closer, to bend above the thing that projected from his skull. It was the hand and wrist from a doll. A big doll. There was a circular flange at its open end, where it rested against the dead man; the sort of flange which permits the rest of the doll, the stuffed cloth body, to be clamped on. The surface of the flesh-colored paint was chipped, eaten away as if by moisture and long abandonment. *Or as if by being buried. . . .*

She touched the tips of the broken fingers. The whole thing came off without any pulling on her part. She almost jumped backward and screamed. Inside the hard composition form was a wadding of paper. And in the short hair at the base of Bart Dewel's skull something silvery gleamed.

Miss Rachel shut her eyes. She felt very ill.

The silvery thing was the eye of a needle, a very big needle, the sort that Mrs. Krythe had brought when she had come to make slip covers for Miriam. The eye of the needle projected from Bart Dewel's skin.

The rest of the needle was buried in his brain.

Someone had made a compact little weapon out of the needle and the hand from the doll. The paper wadding had held the needle firm and the hard composition of which the doll's hand was made had kept the outward end from inflicting any hurt upon the person who had driven it, stiletto-like, into Bart Dewel's brain.

Sharon had retreated into the long room at the front of the house. Her eyes, on Miss Rachel, were wide and sick.

"Tell me what happened," Miss Rachel said. She sat down on a redwood seat and motioned for Sharon to sit by her.

Sharon came forward like a sleepwalker. "We had a date to meet here at one o'clock. I was late." She turned her wrist and a narrow little watch winked in the light. "I found him . . . like that."

Miss Rachel touched her fingers, found them icy. "Why did you agree to meet Dewel here?"

A gray color spread under Sharon's skin. "There were things we had to talk over."

Miss Rachel said impatiently: "Before Miriam's murder you were very cool to this man and ignored his advances. After her death your attitude strangely changed. You seemed afraid of him. You seemed to acknowledge some hold he had over you. In the interview this morning on the terrace there was an understanding between you, an understanding not put into words. I want the truth about it."

Sharon made a cup of her trembling hands and stared into it as though something precious lay there, something which she must guard. Another's freedom perhaps. Another's life.

She shook her head.

Miss Rachel went on, "The only other thing which I recall as frightening you unduly was the story about the doll. I think you knew what that doll meant."

Was Sharon really as pinched, as drained of life, as she seemed? Or was the gray light playing tricks? The eyes that looked unwinking into the hollow of her hands seemed set in enormous sockets.

"And perhaps Mr. Dewel knew the secret of that doll."

"Perhaps he did," Sharon said expressionlessly.

Miss Rachel wanted to shake her.

"I myself recall some unpleasantness about a doll. It must have been some years ago. You were small. Hadn't you once a big doll, a very lovely doll which your father had found somewhere . . . ?" She stopped, trying to chase the elusive memory that connected Ray Hamilton and Sharon with a doll.

Sharon closed her hands tight. A tendon jumped in her wrist.

"Wait. It was your mother's doll," said Miss Rachel. "Your father learned where it was and sent for it for you. And Miriam was angry and jealous. The doll suddenly disappeared. Your father and Miriam quarreled about it."

Sharon didn't answer but the silence in the long room seemed to take on a singing, electric, high-strung quality.

Miss Rachel said in puzzlement: "The doll looks as though it had been *buried.* . . ."

Sharon's voice came out choked and strange. "Please don't say anything like that to anyone else. Especially not to Sheriff Butterworth or Dr. Page. *Please.*"

"Sharon . . . why?"

"I can't tell you." She stood up quickly and walked to the row of windows. She looked almost gaunt inside the strict black dress; she was like a figure of grief, ageless and hopeless. After a moment she spoke quietly. "There's someone below, in the trees. I can see a face. . . . It's a man. No, it's Jerry Krythe. He shouldn't be here."

"Send him away," said Miss Rachel. "Tell him to go to the house and ask Butterworth to come here."

Sharon went out. The opened door let in a breath of manzanita and wet grass and sage. All at once the windows brightened. The fog was lifting; the sun was coming through.

Sharon's attitude of hopelessness was frightening. It implied a deep melancholy insight into the inner workings of the affair, and the acceptance of defeat. Miss Rachel's thoughts went back to the time of Miriam's wedding to Ray Hamilton. Sharon had been a lost little girl; Miss Rachel recalled the tears, the eyes full of frightened questions, the small hot hand inside her own. Sharon had loved her brilliant, handsome father intensely—she had shared him perhaps unwillingly—and after his death in France had come the long grieving, the blight on youth, the black clothing that never let one forget Sharon's mourning.

Ray Hamilton wouldn't have wanted his daughter to behave like this. He was too sane a person, too sensitive to the happiness of others, and—being an artist—too aware of the brevity of the time when one is young. Sharon must know all of this. It occurred to Miss Rachel that Sharon's seeming grief might be something else.

Miriam's reaction to Ray Hamilton's leaving her and his death had been bafflement, fury, a deepening sense of self-blame which she had tried to mask with arrogance and chic.

Sharon's attitude, on the other hand, betrayed no puzzlement as to why her father might have felt impelled to go to France, to die in the debacle at Dunkirk. And yet he had not been the sort of man to go overboard for a cause; if Ray Hamilton had had a fault it had been the self-interest that enabled him to concentrate upon his career.

Strange, Miss Rachel considered, that she had never realized before that Sharon must know why her father had gone as he had.

She sat up straighter on the redwood bench. Sharon had not returned. Suddenly alert, more than a little worried, she went to the door and looked out. Below was the brown flank of the hill. The starveling trees stood dappled in sunlight and the groves beyond were like the dark beginnings of a sea. But she saw no Jerry Krythe, no Sharon.

Perhaps Jerry Krythe had been unwilling to go to Butterworth; perhaps Sharon had not wanted to send him. Most likely she had gone herself with the message.

The sense of strangeness, of aloneness, returned. She had no desire to wait in the house with a dead man. Too, Butterworth might resent her poking into things, being there ahead of him; the tactful thing would be to talk to him later.

On the grove path she found another branch to the pathway. It ended on a well-graveled road. There was no sign of a house, no sound except the rattle and cough of an old car, coming nearer.

Jerry Krythe went by quickly in his little truck. He glanced at her briefly, passing, then stared fiercely at the road.

She walked on in the direction the truck had gone. A man in a blue coupé gave her a lift to the village.

It was a small place, nestled in a valley among the groves with the green majesty of Miriam's hill rising on its other side. There shouldn't be any difficulty about finding her way home. But since she was here she thought she might as well have a look around. At Mrs. Krythe's drapery and notions shop for instance.

The business district took up the south side of a single block. The buildings were haphazard as to architecture and condition. Some were well built, spruce, shining; others were battered and in need of paint. Miss Rachel studied the array: a Mexican combined café and wineshop, two little groceries, a feed and grain store, a pharmacy, Mrs. Krythe's notion store, and a cocktail bar. The cocktail bar was the shiniest of all.

Miss Rachel wondered wistfully if she could investigate the bar without Miss Jennifer's hearing of it. She had long envied the casual male detective of fiction and motion pictures who spent most of his working time at bars and therein picked up all sorts of clues and information.

The door of the bar was open to the sunny afternoon. She took a sidelong glance as she went past. The bartender had his elbows on the counter, facing her. He seemed to be listening to a broadcast from a little radio beside him. The interior was shadowy but at the far end of the bar was a figure which reminded her of Mr. Braudryck.

She looked about the street for his long sleek car and could not find it. Cautiously she turned and walked past again. This time the eye of the bartender followed her. He was a plump redheaded man with a waggish expression. She ignored him, staring past at the other man. The figure raised a glass and emptied it at a gulp. She still couldn't be sure that it was Mr. Braudryck.

Then, at the other side of the building, she saw a walk which seemed to lead to a parking space at the rear. There was even a gray fender sticking out into sight.

She sidled past the door for the third time, staring hard, and suddenly the bartender grinned and raised a hand to beckon to her.

Miss Rachel stopped. She felt as though she might be blushing.

The finger went on wiggling and then he winked, slowly.

Curiosity—the kind Miss Jennifer declares would take Miss Rachel in to explore hell itself—sent her across the threshold and into the pleasantly darkened room with its long bar, a few tables, a silent juke box, and an automatic bowling machine.

The bartender leaned toward her confidingly. "Come closer."

She went closer.

"Have one on the house," he invited with another devilish wink. "Just name it."

Plainly he thought that he was being very funny, inviting a little old white-haired lady in for a drink. Miss Rachel glanced behind her. The street seemed to be empty—at least of Jennifer. She slid up on a stool.

"Thank you so much," she said. "And it'll be an old-fashioned."

He seemed somewhat staggered. For an instant the grin went slack. Then he gravely put out his hand. Miss Rachel took it.

"You're a sport," he said. He squeezed her hand then went off to make the drink.

It *was* Mr. Braudryck at the other end of the bar. He had a bottle of whisky at his elbow—an old, trusted customer evidently—and he was pouring double shots and drinking them, one after another.

In between drinks he stared with a rather belligerent expression into the bar mirror.

If he had seen Miss Rachel come in he was pretending he hadn't.

# CHAPTER ELEVEN

THE COCKTAIL was mellow and smooth. Miss Rachel expressed her appreciation. The bartender warmed to her.

"I'll bet I know who you are," he said. "You're one of the little old—uh—one of the ladies visiting at Mrs. Hamilton's. Aren't you?" He waited for her nod. "I guess you were up there, then, this morning when they found her. Must of been pretty awful."

"You've heard about it?"

"Who hasn't? Lots of excitement over it. It's the first murder I recall around here, except maybe old man Burrows last year, and he was more of an accident. He set a shotgun trap for a chicken thief. Then he forgot and went after eggs. They tried to blame the fellow who'd been getting the chickens but he had an alibi."

As though the murmur of conversation had suddenly pierced his mood of abstraction, Mr. Braudryck turned and noticed Miss Rachel. For an instant—a properly brief instant—he allowed himself to show surprise at finding her there. Then he came, sliding bottle and glass down the bar, and sat down beside her. His long face and his slightly pouched eyes were wise and malicious. "Did you really have to throw me to the wolves like that?"

Miss Rachel batted her eyelashes demurely. "Oh. Did I?"

"You must have made a very fishy talk out of my being on Miriam's terrace at midnight. Butterworth chewed it over like a pup with an old shoe. It was perfectly aboveboard really. Miriam called me in a hurry—she often did—and I came running. She liked to keep her hired help on the jump. It must have helped that inferiority complex of hers like everything."

He was shrewd to have seen that Miriam's pride and arrogance were a bitter mask for something else—for the humiliation of losing Ray Hamilton, for the affront to her jealous, possessive love.

Braudryck poured himself a new drink. "What I really wanted to say, though"—his suave tone roughened a little—"is that I refuse—*refuse,* mind you— to be sacrificed in however noble a cause for somebody else." His gray eyes turned on her with an opalescent hardness. "For dear old Rick. Understand?"

Miss Rachel became surprised. "I'm very fond of Rick but I don't believe I'd sacrifice anyone else in his place if he were guilty of murder."

"Let me buy you another drink," said Mr. Braudryck gently, much as the wolf must have spoken to Little Red Ridinghood. "And listen to a few facts straight from life. Rick's dad, old man Flanders, wasn't any moron. He was clever as hell and as grasping as an ape. He wanted to be good to Miriam, naturally. He left her that oversized hotel for a home and he protected her groves by providing in his will that other funds were to be drawn upon if the groves were threatened. They haven't been, incidentally. Good times changed all that. But Flanders might almost have been looking into the future and seeing someone like Ray Hamilton there. He made sure that none of the money could go to anyone but Miriam or his son. His son Rick."

"But I don't see——"

"In these last weeks Miriam was on a hunt of some kind, and she was furious. She was after somebody. I think there'd been a little spite work on the sly, and you know how that would have affected her. She had made up her mind to punish whoever it was when she caught him. And when Miriam punished she flayed alive."

Miss Rachel's throat was dry. "Not Rick——"

The deep gleam in his gray eye could have been a touch of pity. Or it, could have been satisfaction. "Rick and Sharon."

Sharon had said, Miss Rachel remembered, that Miriam suspected her in the matter of the damage to the fuchsias. She had kept Rick's name out of it. And today, in the long studio room of Ray Hamilton's house, there had been the odd air of protecting someone else. . . . *Rick?*

As though he saw the memory, the unwilling belief in Miss Rachel's face, Mr. Braudryck turned casual. "The scheme Miriam had worked out, the method she outlined to me last night, was pretty cute. I saw at once why she had chosen first to tackle Rick. He had something she could get. There were to have been some manipulations of profits, claims of spoilage and infestations of trees, even sales of land at a loss. Funds from the Flanders estate were to be drawn upon to cover. Of course it would have taken time and a lot of careful work. Maybe a little bribery in the right places."

Miss Rachel was sitting very straight on the stool. "But the result would have been that Rick was a pauper."

"In debt even," said Braudryck. "Miriam was a damned thorough thief."

To Miss Rachel's taste her new drink had a strange flatness. The bartender, though he must be listening, was scrubbing the bar as if he were mad at it.

She said, "But Rick couldn't have known this. She wouldn't have warned him."

"She was pretty mad. Mad enough to be careless. On the terrace I thought about warning her to keep her voice down and then didn't bother. I didn't want her jumping down my throat. But voices do carry clearly out of doors."

A new idea made Miss Rachel's heart thump, hard. "Have you told Sheriff Butterworth all this?"

Braudryck looked into the bar mirror enigmatically. "I'm waiting."

She played his game, though she hated it. "For what?"

"I want to know how Miriam was killed. Old Butterworth's fumbling around trying to find out. He'll do it eventually. I've got a hunch"—he poured a drink—"just a hunch, that when they find out *how* she was killed I'm going to have a hell of a punch line telling them *why*."

She felt fear stifling her thoughts, wondered if Braudryck could read her feelings in her face. Was the man actually that smart? Did he have any idea of the impact of what he had told her, when it should be combined with the truth about the tractor—the tractor which Rick had been repairing in the barn? *The tractor that Rick could have found and started in the dark?*

For it had been dark, there where Miriam had died. She remembered the brief flicker of Checkers's match in that black cavern hung with shadows. If Rick had waited until Checkers and Mrs. Krythe had gone, knowing that Miriam had slipped in and hidden . . .

But, her thoughts added irrelevantly, if Miriam was already there she must have heard, as Miss Rachel had, the plotting between the two. . . . She turned to Braudryck suddenly. "Didn't you ask me something about Mrs. Krythe when we met on the terrace?"

He didn't meet her glance. "Did I? I guess I've forgotten."

"You asked me if Mrs. Krythe had been at Miriam's house yesterday."

He drank, and stared into the little glass. "Oh, just curiosity. Miriam had a feud with Dave Krythe once. Didn't work out so good for him."

"And you knew—or perhaps Miriam knew and told you—that Dave Krythe had just died. What did he die of?"

He cradled the bottle, poured gently. He even added a bit to Miss Rachel's glass, filling it. "Tuberculosis. Overwork, really. He fought Miriam the only way he knew, by working like a dog to raise money for lawyers." The gray eyes were the color of steel. "That was a fool's way. The way Rick did it now——"

"*Don't say that!*"

He smiled at his whisky, a lopsided, unfunny smile. "Miss Rachel! I didn't know you cared!"

She pushed down the mounting panic, forced herself to sample the drink. Reinforced as Braudryck had fixed it, it was now a powerful mixture. She found the bartender's eye on her and there was worry in it. "Would Rick have any motive—as you reconstruct things—for killing somebody else also?"

Again the grin, wider, real humor in it. "Were you there long enough to size up the situation between Sharon and Bart?"

She just stared, her heart gone dead.

"You were?" he said mockingly, as if reading her thought. "Then you know what I mean."

The long needle, the horrible needle . . . Miss Rachel cried: "*Rick wouldn't!*"

He held up a finger from the hand that cradled the whisky bottle. "I'm not saying that he would. I'm just not going to be a burnt offering on the family altar. See?"

His lean gray leg, swinging from the bar stool, was opposite her toe. She ached to kick him in the shin.

"Go on," he urged. "Kick away."

He wasn't psychic. His eyes had followed hers and he had read the mutiny in her face.

He went on: "As for throwing suspicion on Mrs. Krythe or Jerry—well, I can't see any future in it. Jerry's ideas of right and wrong seem pretty hazy, and he has been in trouble. . . . But picking on a widow's kid won't help Butterworth, come election, and he knows it. And Mrs. Krythe's the weepy, wishy-washy type nobody will believe harm of." He leaned toward her as if confidingly. "So I'd just give that up."

For a moment a furious anger swept over her and thoughts of mayhem flitted in her mind. Then she forced herself to realize that Braudryck was simply judging her by himself, figuring that she had done what he would have: covering for somebody you liked; callously giving the law another victim; planting clues, and so forth.

*Planting clues* . . . It would serve Braudryck right if somebody planted a few on him.

Nothing seriously incriminating of course. Just the fin off a red herring for Butterworth to sniff at while the truth could be found in the mass of evidence that seemed to point at Rick.

She finished her drink and slid off the stool. The floor was a bit unsteady and the light that came in through the door unexpectedly bright. Of course she'd been sitting facing the gloomy interior. Perhaps her legs were somewhat tired from being swung from the stool.

She said hypocritically to Mr. Braudryck, "I hope that everything turns out well for you." She meant to smile wisely and found instead that she had giggled.

The bartender eyed her with concern. "You okay, ma'am?"

"I'm perfectly—I'm fine," she rebuked him. She went out, turning in the direction she would have taken to go home. But her mind was on the parking lot at the rear of the bar. She found a weed-grown space between two buildings and scrambled through it, gathering foxtails and stickers and frightening a horned toad and a couple of lizards. In the rear of the little block of business houses was a cleared space for loading and parking. Beyond was a rising hill and what seemed to be an abandoned excavation.

Mr. Braudryck's Cadillac was behind the building containing the bar. She found it unlocked. His scarf, white with a gray border, lay on the seat. This she passed over as too obvious. In the glove compartment she sorted through a flashlight, a pint of bourbon, a racing sheet, an unopened carton of Camels, and three little green leather make-up kits labeled in gold lettering, "Blonde, Brunette, Redhead." In each were make-up materials, powder and rouge and lipstick. The lipsticks were used up. In each case a little flat pocket was empty. At the very back of the compartment she discovered two little folders of matches. They had been made for Braudryck, possibly presented in a pack as a gift. On the cream-colored paper back was a monogram, a little *E* and *T*, a big ornate *B*.

She remembered seeing Mr. Braudryck's signature somewhere. His name was Everett Thomas. Good.

She stuffed the little match folders into her pocket and started to leave.

A hollow metallic scratching caused her to pause, to look about carefully.

Beyond the parking space the land rose to a hill. The area to Miss Rachel's right had been gouged out and carried away, leaving a red scar now covered thinly with scrubby bushes and dead grass. Someone had had a stab at running a brickyard. She saw an abandoned kiln, some tumbled piles of scrapped brick, and two great rusty boilers with crooked smokestacks on the verge of falling over. The hollow metallic scratching sound seemed to come from them.

She waited, puzzled, a little uneasy. And then, as a newly hatched chick from its shell, Miss Jennifer Murdock crawled from the opening of one boiler, dusted herself fretfully, and went to peer into the black interior of the other. She was wearing a black alpaca coat over her dark green taffeta. She carried a flashlight in one hand and her purse in the other.

Miss Rachel was seized with horrid doubts as to her own sanity, until she remembered the drinks she had had. She had always understood that during the latter stages of an alcoholic orgy one saw unusual, even nightmarish, visions.

Miss Rachel, being a moderate tippler both by taste and by the watchfulness of her sister, had never had so much as a hangover. It seemed to her now that the two drinks she had had at the bar scarcely constituted a jag. Still the phantom of Miss Jennifer scrambling from one boiler to vanish into the maw of the other was on a plane of nightmare almost beyond belief.

She fled the place, to stand panting and dizzy on the sidewalk. The village, drowsy under the warm afternoon sun, seemed a harmless and pretty place. Miss Rachel looked earnestly for flitting shapes and found none.

She went on in the direction of Mrs. Krythe's little store. It was a small white frame building with two big front windows filled with notions and samples of drapery materials. A lettered sign above the door said: SLIP COVERS CUSTOM-MADE.

A much smaller sign at the rear of one of the show windows read: DOLLS DRESSED AND REPAIRED.

A little doll in a fluffy pink-sprigged dress sat beside the sign.

On a sudden urge Miss Rachel tried to walk into the shop. The door was locked. She peered in through the pane in its upper section. She saw a glass counter filled with trimming materials: flowers, feathers, spangles; a rack of ribbons; a sewing machine; a long table used for measuring and cutting. Scissors lay open on it, and the scraps of a dark blue brocade.

There was no sign of Mrs. Krythe and no pinned-up notice to explain her absence during what must be business hours.

Perhaps the common knowledge of her husband's death was notice enough. Perhaps she was away doing what Checkers had advised—seeing about Jerry's interest in his father's estate.

Only, of course, Mrs. Krythe didn't have to worry any longer about the omnivorous greed of Miriam Hamilton.

It popped into Miss Rachel's head suddenly that Jerry Krythe should know how to run a tractor. He owned a little truck, he did odd jobs and ran errands for the ranchers.

"I'm not," she said to herself, "making a burnt offering of Jerry." But Mr. Braudryck's hints had left a sense of guilt.

She found another weed-grown passage and went through it with the idea of finding out whether Mrs. Krythe's living quarters were at the rear and whether she was in them. At the last moment, remembering, she stopped and peered from the shadows at the abandoned brickyard.

Even as she looked the phantom of Miss Jennifer put forth

its head (wearing as in life the seventeen-year-old black toque) from the second boiler and surveyed the surroundings warily.

It was a frighteningly vivid nightmare. Miss Rachel could see the gleam of Miss Jennifer's eyes and the shine of her unpowdered nose. The black toque was spotted with rust.

Miss Rachel tried to scream and managed a strangled squeak. Then she turned and ran blindly. The stalk of a big weed caught her ankle, wound tight, held.

She fell flat on her face.

For a moment there was breathless pain, darkness, surging nausea. Someone came into the passage and bent over her, helping her to sit up. The cold lip of a bottle touched her mouth. She smelled whisky.

A soothing voice said, "Drink."

# CHAPTER TWELVE

Miss Rachel gasped, "I've already had too much! I'm seeing things. . . ."

"Nobody ever had too much," said the soothing voice.

She sat still while breath struggled back into her body. The dizziness melted away. She saw that her comforter was Joe Dewel. "You've had quite a tumble. Knock your breath out?" He urged the bottle toward her. "Here. Have a snort."

He was oddly changed. True, he was as usual under the influence of alcohol; but the half-hidden look of worry and anxiety was gone. He was round, jovial, easy. Of course, she thought pityingly, he couldn't have heard yet about his brother's death.

Or could he?

He bent over her. "Running from somebody?"

"A—a ghost."

He laughed and the sound was genuine, confident. "Seeing things, huh? I've seen 'em too, in my time. I've even looked myself over for snake bites when I was sober. Well, if you won't have one . . ." He put the bottle to his own lips and took a long gurgle. There was no pretense now, no smell of breath scent or hiding the bottle. Mr. Joe Dewel acted much as if he had just lost a jailer.

She got to her feet and they walked to the street. She thought about trying to break the news to him about Bart Dewel and then gave it up. For some reason he seemed happy; let him stay so for a little while. But she still worried about the phantom. "It couldn't have been real. It had to be a . . . a . . ."

"Pink elephant?" he offered.

"I'm sure that even Jennifer's shadow image would resent being called a pink elephant," she told him. "It's much too gay. Let's just say hallucination." She brushed dust and foxtails from her skirts. "Anyway, it couldn't have been my sister."

The easy smile stayed on his face but his eyes grew curious. "Oh? Where?"

"In the boilers. The old boilers on the hill. She wouldn't be crawling from one to the other—not Jennifer."

"Well, suppose I have a look and find out if I'm seeing things too. You can wait here if you'd like."

Miss Rachel didn't wait; she knew a surer way of laying the ghost—or whatever it was. She hurried past the last of the little store buildings and struck out on a graveled path for the top of Miriam's hill. It was a stiff climb. The afternoon sunlight had brought out the smells of fresh-turned earth and orange blossoms. Trees hemmed the path with a green wall. At what would be about the halfway mark was a little pergola on a steep point, hedged in with honeysuckle and wild pink roses. Miss Rachel went into the pergola and sat down on a white board bench.

Here she could see the valley spread out below, the toy houses of the village, the shining roads that led to it, even a patch of the brown hill where Ray Hamilton had had his studio.

No one moved in the scene below. The village seemed asleep,

the roads empty. The green groves spread away in all directions like a sea. The bubbling song of a meadow lark and the hum of bees were the only interruptions to the silence. Tall eucalypti, planned in narrow rows where the wind might strike, moved lazily under the touch of a little breeze. It was an utterly beautiful view. Again Miss Rachel had the sharp, frightening sense of flowering beauty covering something hideous and corrupt.

The dark rich land had been scrouged from other people, acre by acre. The shadow of Miriam's greed had crept over valley and hill. Little people had submitted, or they had fought, but in the end they had gone. Miriam had remained.

Was this the thing which was frightening—this ruthless land hunger which had rolled like a juggernaut over the mangled lives of other people? Or was it something subtler . . . and more monstrous?

A chill seemed to have risen out of the valley. Miss Rachel went on toward the house. She passed the swimming pool and entered by way of the terrace. She had a ghost to lay. In Jennifer's room she fully expected to lay it. Jennifer's tongue might be wagging briskly with remarks about Miss Rachel's snooping, but that would be welcome after the dread vision of the brickyard.

Jennifer's embroidery was folded neatly on the bed. On a chaise done in purple-and-white taffeta lay Samantha, sleeping, her black head tucked between her paws, her nose twitching over a dream mouse.

Miss Rachel explored the closet. Jennifer's alpaca coat and the seventeen-year-old hat were gone.

She remembered that Jennifer had been a bit mysterious earlier in the day. She'd said something about wanting time to think, and she had refused to say what the thinking was to be about—

unusual for Jennifer, who usually thought about righteous things and talked freely about them to her sister.

The cat awoke and stretched and then started to sharpen her claws on the taffeta cushion. Miss Rachel caught her up and took her into the hall. A maid, scurrying past with a vacuum cleaner, paused long enough to answer Miss Rachel's question. "I haven't seen her, ma'am. Not since lunch."

*Lunch* . . . No wonder two drinks had made her giddy. She took the cat off to the kitchen, where the cook gave them a cold, flattened soufflé, stony buns, and creamed crab with a slightly burned flavor. There was no indication that the cook had heard of the second murder. She was somewhat calmer and less talkative than she had been earlier.

The kitchen clock gave the time as a quarter of four.

"Mrs. Hamilton always supervised the menus, ma'am," the cook said as Miss Rachel prepared to leave. "Would you care to suggest something?"

"What do you have on hand?" said Miss Rachel practically.

"There's a smoked turkey in the storeroom."

"Have that then."

"What about vegetables?"

"Boil some potatoes and open a can of peas."

"Mrs. Hamilton always liked things done up nicely, ma'am."

"Sprinkle parsley on the potatoes and cream the peas then."

"What about dessert? What wine shall I serve with the turkey? Shouldn't we have a sauce?"

"Burgundy is a nice wine," said Miss Rachel thoughtfully. She had once brazenly brought a bottle home to have with meals, but Jennifer had retaliated with such long and fervent graces that the food had been cold by the time they got around to eating it.

Even burgundy couldn't compensate for leathery steak. "As for the dessert and the sauce, I'll leave that to you."

She explored the house, searching for Jennifer. She found Miriam's private little theater, lonely and dim, smelling of furniture polish and leather upholstery. There were six rows of deeply cushioned seats, forty-eight in all. Miriam couldn't have gathered forty-eight friends at any time during her life.

The chairs facing the little stage had a waiting, expectant look which made Miss Rachel nervous. She went on, the cat following. Another room she investigated was fitted out as a business office. Here was no pretense of fun or relaxation; the room was imbued with the grim business of land grabbing. There was a large, bare, glass-topped desk, several steel filing cabinets, a wall map showing old Mr. Gordon's original holdings, and another bigger map showing Miriam's additions. On tiptoe, Miss Rachel read the finely inked lettering on the various plots. A green square to the north of the village was lettered faintly in pencil:

KRYTHE
11.6 A.
?

Here Miriam's impatient greed had overreached itself, counting a section before its owners had been completely cheated out of it.

Such a piece of ground should be worth fighting for. Figuring at a low price of two thousand dollars an acre, the property would be worth better than twenty-two thousand. Probably in these times the value was closer to thirty or thirty-five thousand. With the income from her little grove, Mrs. Krythe wouldn't need to keep a store.

In spite of Braudryck's remarks about a burnt offering, could Miriam's death have come so opportunely for anyone as it had for Mrs. Krythe?

She had left the door open behind her. She noted a startled move on the part of her cat. Sheriff Butter-worth had walked in quietly. He came and stood behind her. "Find something?" The tone of his voice told her that he was angry and baffled and trying not to show either.

"Nothing you wouldn't have seen," she said.

"Why did you run off before I got to the Hamilton place?"

"I was nervous."

"Where did you go?"

"To the village, then up the hill to the house."

"Meet anybody?"

"I talked to Mr. Braudryck and to Mr. Joe Dewel in the village." She decided to omit mention of the mirage of Jennifer.

"Did you tell them about Bart's murder?"

"No."

His square face remained tight and unreadable. Suddenly he moved toward the map and put a big finger on the name of Krythe. "Mrs. Hamilton had her eye on that land. She held the mortgage, though Dave Krythe didn't know she'd bought his note from the original owner. All at once he was up to his neck in lawsuits. A fellow claimed that Dave had let his irrigation water overflow and flood out some bean land. He was burning brush when the fire got out of control in some strange way and burned a hundred acres of another man's pasture. Other odd things happened and they all ended in suits. Krythe tried to borrow more money on his land and ran up against a stone wall. That stone wall was Mrs. Hamilton. The men suing Krythe were her stooges."

Miss Rachel flushed. "How could she?"

He moved around to lean against the top of a filing cabinet. The hat he held in his hand he tossed to Miriam's desk. "She was the grabbingest woman I ever knew, always. But later there'd been something more, something about her husband leaving the way he did. I used to see her tearing around the country in her big cars, going like a bat out of hell if you'll excuse the expression, and I knew something was wrong."

Miss Rachel interrupted. "This affair about getting Krythe's land—did it happen before or after Ray Hamilton went away?"

He was silent. The skin under his eyes drew tight as though he were staring against a strong glare. Then he said, "About that time, I think. It began and Mr. Hamilton went off to Europe. You think the scheme might have sickened him, sent him away from her?"

"Something happened which made Ray Hamilton want to leave. Miriam always suspected that he had wangled the European assignment with some of her money, that it was just an excuse to get away. I've always wondered what might have caused him to go. I think that's what mystified and angered Miriam so—he left her and before she could reach him to patch things up he was killed. Of course, as you say, Miriam had been a land grabber from childhood. It was born in her, since she was her father's daughter. But Ray Hamilton may not have realized this for a long while. He was an artist, perhaps also an idealist. He had an intense desire to perfect his painting technique, to be famous."

Butterworth was studying her from under bushy eyebrows. "So maybe he didn't catch on to the dirty work until something really raw came along, something as raw as the Krythe deal which set everybody in the valley talking about it."

"It's quite possible. In that case, would Miriam have blamed the Krythes for his going?"

He didn't answer her question. Perhaps he was remembering, as Braudryck had suggested, that picking on the Krythes wouldn't help him, come election time. He motioned toward the desk and the chairs that faced it. "We might as well sit down. As for this item about the Krythes—now that we're on that subject, I want to hear about Mrs. Krythe's big needle."

So he wasn't shying off the possibility of the widow and her boy being involved. Miss Rachel hunted about for a safe, non-committal answer. What she had thought to herself about the Krythes was her business. Oddly, she suddenly felt exactly as Mr. Braudryck had seemed to feel regarding burnt offerings. "Mrs. Krythe was here at the house yesterday. I understood that she had come to do some slip covers for Miriam. She came out on the terrace about dusk."

"Who else was there?" asked Butterworth quickly.

"When we first noticed that Mrs. Krythe had dropped the needle there were five of us on the terrace. The two Dewel brothers, Rick, my sister, and myself."

"Sharon tells me she didn't see the needle when she returned to the terrace after showing Mrs. Krythe to the other entry, that the first she heard of it was at dinner."

Miss Rachel bent, picked up her cat, and sat it in her lap, stroking the black silky ears. "I'm trying to remember. I don't believe I noticed just when the needle disappeared."

"Who was the first to leave the terrace?"

There was no evading this point. "Rick was. He had some matter he wanted to take up with Miriam. Besides——" She stopped in horror. Absently, she had been about to mention Bart Dewel's sly hints about getting married, the little rhyme about needles and pins, the abrupt angry way Rick had gone off into the house. "Besides," she finished lamely, "it was getting late."

"And then what?"

"Sharon came back and suggested we go indoors. In the hall we came across Jerry Krythe talking to Rick. He had been supposed to call here for his mother and he had missed her."

"And presumably this needle was left out on the terrace?"

Miss Rachel wrinkled her usually smooth brow. It seemed now that it would have been unlike Miss Jennifer, the meticulous needlewoman, to leave such a noticeable needle out in the night air to rust. She explained this point to Butterworth.

"So perhaps the needle had already been hidden?" he suggested.

She shook her head. "No one could have picked up the needle and run it into a coat lapel or a pocket lining without being seen. It must have been brushed off the table to the floor." And still in her mind's eye the yellow-brick paving had held no shine of steel. There had been the wrought-iron table, the ornamental chairs. And of course Sharon's typewriter case. . . .

Her heart lurched. She was remembering Sharon, this morning, sitting suddenly still with her hand holding the catch of her typewriter case, looking in at something under the lid.

She felt the heavy pounding of her own pulse, the breathless ache in her throat. She looked surreptitiously at Sheriff Butterworth. His eyes on her own were wise and ruthless.

"I'm just trying to get at the truth about the murder of these two people," he said reasonably. "I want to know who caught Mrs. Hamilton behind that door inside the barn and backed the tractor up to crush her. I want to find out who killed Bart Dewel when he was sitting in Hamilton's old studio with a fountain pen in his hand and a blank piece of paper in front of him. I want to run down the person who had that clever idea of using Mrs. Krythe's needle and a doll's arm for a weapon." He leaned forward and put a big hand on the arm of Miss Rachel's chair. "But you aren't helping. Every time you remember some clue that might point to Sharon Hamilton you close up like a clam."

"Everybody in this case," said Miss Rachel, "is psychic. Everybody except me."

# CHAPTER THIRTEEN

"I'M NOT a bit psychic," said Butterworth coldly. "I figured out where that needle must have been hidden when I talked to Sharon. We talked about the terrace, the people on it, the furnishings, and when we'd get around to that typewriter case she'd shy and stumble and yet she couldn't help mentioning it. She was afraid I'd guess the needle had been hidden there, so she tried being casual—only she couldn't. The fear was in her voice. Now I don't know that Sharon hid the needle there; it seems more likely that someone else did. But if she didn't hide the needle *she knows who did.*"

"Or thinks she knows," corrected Miss Rachel, looking him in the eye.

Butterworth drew his lips up wryly. "I can't help but believe that she's protecting Rick Flanders. I'm not such a fool that I can't see how they feel about each other and I know just what an ass Bart Dewel was making of himself over Sharon. Gossip gets around in these parts."

Miss Rachel asked abruptly, "Why did you say that Bart Dewel had been writing something?"

"Hmmm? Oh, he had a fountain pen under his right hand

and a sheet of note paper had slipped to the floor under the table. These could mean that he had known something about the murder of Mrs. Hamilton and was writing it down. Don't you think so?"

She tried very hard to look ignorant.

He went on, "I figure Bart as a kind of blackmailer. He was the smart-alecky, go-getter type, too damned brassy to be scared, too stupid to take care of himself when things got dangerous. Maybe he was trying to get money for this information. Maybe he was trying to get something else—a hold on Sharon for instance. After all there was some reason he wanted to talk to her privately. Just suppose for example he'd said, 'Look, Sharon, here's a bit of evidence that makes things look bad for Rick. How about being nice, huh?'"

The obnoxiousness of Mr. Bart Dewel seemed to fill the room. She remembered the strange interview on the terrace this morning, and Dewel's veiled words: *"There were signs of the storm from way back, weren't there? . . . Threats . . . One of the maids was screaming gibberish to Butterworth about a doll. . . ."*

The doll . . .

*That was it.* His mention of the doll had made Sharon frightened and docile.

"Then suppose," Butterworth was saying, "that when Sharon met him alone in that house she just couldn't stand him."

The hand with which Miss Rachel stroked her cat was trembling a little.

He made an easy, relaxed gesture with one hand. "Now why don't you just go ahead and tell me what you're thinking?"

"I can't believe that Sharon went to her old home, talked with Bart Dewel there, quarreled, and thrust a needle into his brain as he started to betray Rick to the police."

He nodded contentedly, waiting for more.

"That's all," she said firmly. "I haven't anything else to say."

He straightened slowly in his chair, measuring her. When he spoke his voice came out clipped and angry. "You were with Sharon, weren't you, when she made this date to meet Dewel?"

Someone had told him this. "Yes, I was."

"What was said then?"

Anger rose in her to meet his own, and she repressed it. This was the time for a cool head. "Very little was said. He seemed to want to be helpful and Sharon told him there were matters to be settled in regard to her father's estate, now that Miriam was dead. There were papers, I think, at her father's house."

"The place is bare. How did she act toward Dewel—resentful?"

"She seemed unhappy. That was natural, wasn't it?"

"She hadn't liked Bart Dewel at all, she used to treat him with a very thin courtesy. I've seen that. Now why would she want him to help her in her personal affairs?"

Miss Rachel rose with dignity. "I think you've made up your mind in regard to all this. You're convinced Sharon met Bart Dewel for some discussion, some blackmail in regard to Miriam's death. You think Sharon or Rick murdered Dewel to conceal that evidence." She paused at the door. His eyes had followed her, narrow with enmity. "So why question me? All you need in your methods are a closed mind, a pair of handcuffs, and a length of rubber hose."

She went out and his muttered anger drifted after her.

She went to her bedroom and sat down there until the hot feeling inside her breast had cooled a little. The cat, ears set at an angle indicating curiosity, sniffed at the bathroom door. Miss Rachel went quietly and turned the knob. Miss Jennifer, at the gleaming black washbasin, was running water onto her hands.

On the end of her unpowdered nose was a streak of rust. On the great Byzantine bed in the room beyond lay the black alpaca coat, the toque, the purse, and the flashlight.

"So it wasn't nightmare after all," murmured Miss Rachel. "Jennifer, are you quite well? I observed your antics in the boilers."

Miss Jennifer jumped in surprise and chagrin, and let her hand get too close to the faucet. Water sprayed the bathroom. She wiped it up fiercely with a coral-colored towel. Then she marched out, and just before the bedroom door closed Miss Rachel heard something like, "You aren't the only fish in the sea!"

Miss Rachel crossed the bathroom and tapped on Jennifer's door. "Let me talk to you. Please."

"You're not going to pump me," said Jennifer; her voice through the door was muffled.

"What's in those boilers?" demanded Miss Rachel.

"Are you kidding?"

This terse and pointed colloquialism was so unlike Jennifer that Miss Rachel retreated in confusion to her own room.

She was tempted to explore the boilers for herself, since obviously some strange mystery surrounded them, but other matters demanded attention. Butterworth had admitted that he knew now how Miriam had died. Was there some significance in how he had found out?

She went out again into the late afternoon, the cat following.

The barn was still shadowy, still full of musty coolness. The tractor sat undisturbed in its litter of tools. Miss Rachel climbed up into the seat and poked buttons and pulled levers. The motor sputtered raggedly and died. She did more poking. The motor roared; the chassis quivered. She was just about to let out the clutch lever when Rick came running in from the corral.

"Good God, you scared me half to death! What the devil are you trying to do?"

"Does it run?" she asked innocently.

"Of course it runs. It runs like a stripe-backed ape." He shut off the motor and then went to glance behind the folded door to the lath house. "It must have been horrible for Miriam. Do you know she was crushed behind this thing?"

"Oh."

"It came to me all at once this morning. I'd come out here to finish work on the tractor and found the ignition on. Then I saw where the tire tracks went back and where they had skidded a little, close to the wall. Then there was the door, divided the way it is. If Miriam were caught back of it she'd have been just as they found her, body crushed but nothing done to her face because her head would reach above the lower panel."

"And you told Butterworth this?"

"That's right."

"When?"

"Oh, a little while ago. Right after he got back from the Hamilton place."

"Did he, in return, tell you why he had been there?"

Rick's eyes avoided hers. "Something about some papers of Sharon's, wasn't it?"

She studied his square, homely, likable face. "Rick, don't pretend."

"All right, I won't. Sharon told me what happened. But I want Butterworth to break the news in his own way. I want him to think he's tangling me up. Then I'll have an idea of how to fight back."

She looked at him from her perch on the tractor. "Did Jennifer give you my message?"

His face changed. He put a clenched fist on the hood of the tractor. "You too?" he asked quietly.

"No, Rick, not me." No use telling Rick she had endured Mr. Braudryck's odious company and been frightened to death by Jennifer on his account. "I'm on your side. You've got to believe that."

He met her gaze frankly. "It's because of Sharon then. I've always been a surly lunk with nothing much to say and no signs of social graces."

"No, Rick," she said earnestly. "Haven't we always been friends? Don't you remember how you used to explain things like main bearings and piston rods to me? I wouldn't have cared for you if you'd been a—a lounge lizard."

"Lounge lizard?" said Rick.

"I've lived through so many different eras of slang that I sometimes get them mixed up. Anyway, we need an awful lot of young men like you now, Rick. Men who aren't afraid of work and grease, and who don't worry about holding their teacups correctly."

"Nuts," said Rick modestly and without offense.

"But about this message I gave Jennifer——"

"To go to the Hamilton place? I went, you know."

She suddenly felt cold and weary. "Was Bart Dewel there?"

"You might as well hear the whole story. I wasn't sure what your message meant. But Joe had met Sharon on the terrace and noticed which path she took from below the pool. He thought she looked worried. Of course he didn't know about Bart. Well, when I reached the studio the door was about half open. Inside I could see Dewel kissing Sharon, standing in the middle of the floor, and she was hanging in his arms like a rag doll, like a little kid that's too afraid to scream. I—well, I went kind of crazy. I bellowed something and charged in and when the haze cleared up a little Dewel was crouched in the doorway to the kitchen holding his jaw and I could hear myself breathing as if I'd run a long way."

A sudden fear that someone might be listening shot through Miss Rachel's mind. She held her breath. From the lath house came the sound of a leaky faucet dripping water into a tin container—a watering pot perhaps. Out in the corral a family of blackbirds was scolding her cat.

"I took Sharon away from there, brought her back here to the house, and made her promise to lie down. She looked—excuse the word, I admitted I'm an oaf—she looked like hell."

"She looked like hell when I saw her at the studio," said Miss Rachel absently, remembering the sunken eyes, the paperish skin, the cupped trembling hands into which Sharon had stared.

"Now Sharon admits that she went back to the place after I left her. She says that she tried to lie down, as she had promised, and that she spent a little time looking for you. Perhaps she wanted advice about how to treat Dewel. It was during this time the man must have been killed."

In a cold, clear moment Miss Rachel saw why Sharon must think that Rick had committed the murder. There had been the fierce, bitter fight, Rick had taken her away in blazing anger and warned her to stay put. Then—as Sharon must see things—Rick had gone back to do the killing.

Rick, it was true, might be the type of man who would, under the stress of tremendous emotion, batter or even shoot another man to death. He had had after all a long apprenticeship in killing in the Solomons. But he was hardly the type to contrive so weird a weapon as that Dewel had been killed with, or to creep up silently and thrust it into the man's brain.

And so . . . whose crime was this?

Why, for instance, use the doll's arm? Why not make a handle for the needle out of wood?

His words interrupted. "Sharon doesn't want me to admit being near the place. I don't know though. Surely they can't put me away for something I didn't do."

"The police are notoriously in a hurry when they need a culprit," she said.

The blackbirds, busy and raucous and angry at the cat, were suddenly silent. Samantha came to stand in the doorway, to look backward and twitch her tail at some sight in the distance.

"Someone's coming," said Miss Rachel, getting down hastily from the seat of the tractor.

Sheriff Butterworth's big businesslike figure strolled toward them as though he had all the time in the world. The sky above was pale and smoky, fading with twilight. The trees were subtly darker, the furrows shadowy. The corral fence had taken on an unearthly whiteness. A young bird called and the sound was ruffled and sleepy.

The sheriff stood in the doorway. "I'd like to talk with you, Flanders."

"Sure," said Rick. "Come on in."

There was little patience in the look Butterworth gave Miss Rachel.

"I was going anyway," she said snippily.

"Then you'll excuse us," said Butterworth.

She was at the door, almost through it, when she caught some movement in the recesses of the lath house. She turned, hesitated. Butterworth watched her stonily.

Against vine-grown latticework the figure of Checkers moved from one shelf of potted plants to another. He was a shadow among other shadows, soundless, unhurrying. There was a little watering pot in one hand. With the other hand he explored the potted soil for signs of dryness. The little fuchsia blossoms, red stars and snowy petticoats, winked in the dim light.

Butterworth moved casually to a point where he could see Checkers at his work. "On the other hand, Flanders, suppose we talk on our way over to the old Hamilton place. You were there today, I take it."

"That's right," said Rick.

When they had gone Miss Rachel went back through the barn and walked down the soggy path between the fuchsias. Checkers must have heard her step and listened to it for a moment without seeming to. He suddenly set down the watering pot and turned his near-blind eyes toward her. "Miss Murdock?"

She wondered how much he had heard of her conversation with Rick. But there was a more important question, one she must ask at once. "Checkers . . . if someone wanted to bury something near by, something fairly big, what would be a good spot?"

He stood silent, his face shadowed and expressionless, his form bent as a curled leaf.

She went on thoughtfully, putting her ideas into words. "The ground in the groves is kept cultivated. It wouldn't do. And a disturbed spot near the driveway or around the flower beds would be noticed. You see, this . . . object . . . has to be disinterred now and then."

Something flitted across his seamed face: alarm or surprise or perhaps even a curious kind of fun. "Disinterred, ma'am? Sounds like a body, sort of. I think you mean Miss Sharon's doll. Dolls don't need buryin', not as much as your cat would."

She found words again after an instant of stunned surprise. “Do you know about Sharon’s doll?”

“It’s an ugly story and you wouldn’t want to hear it, ma’am.” He was sliding past, soundless and wavering as a ghost. “I’m not going to tell it to you anyway. Good night.”

# CHAPTER FOURTEEN

She stood looking after him as he moved away, too surprised to think of something with which to keep him. He stooped and opened a low little door in the lath work. The door was marked with a bright bit of nailed-up tin, part of a can; Miss Rachel noted that many corners of tables in the place were marked likewise. Checkers's footsteps died into silence.

Checkers knew the story of Sharon's doll. He didn't seem to think that it was being kept buried. What was it he had said? . . . *"Dolls don't need buryin', not as much as your cat would."*

She wondered if there had been a vague threat there of harm to Samantha. The words had sounded, however, more like an impromptu comparison, as though his eye had happened to fall on the cat as he was speaking.

Samantha, black as ink, was under the potting table, deep in shadow. She was staring into what must be a mouse burrow.

Was Checkers really as blind as he seemed?

His face lacked expression, as a blind person's might be expected to. He seemed to move by instinct. He had *felt* the earth in the pots, not *looked* to see if it were moist.

Later in the evening, at dinner, her mind still mulled over the point. She and Jennifer went into Miriam's dining room together. The crystal chandelier that Miriam had had brought from Europe before the war shone on the white napery and woke dark reflections in the mahogany and in the decanter of wine on the buffet. Sheriff Butterworth and Sharon were near the buffet. There was the feeling that they had been talking together and that Butterworth had stopped to see who was coming in. Sharon stood stiffly, her face turned from Butterworth, her eyes big and dark with strain.

The sheriff spoke a polite greeting to the two little old ladies.

Rick and Mr. Braudryck came in a moment afterward. Rick, as usual when he put on more formal clothes, looked leaner and more adult. His nod to Butterworth was brief. Evidently their trip to the Hamilton place had not improved the friendship.

Mr. Braudryck's baggy eyes showed the effects of his afternoon with the bottle. They were red-veined. His skin was sallow. The hand he put out to a chair back was shaky. But his greetings for the others were polite, casual.

Miss Rachel counted places at the table. Eight. There were two more yet to arrive.

The consommé had been served and taken away before Joe Dewel came in, thanked Sharon for being kind enough to invite him to dinner, apologized for being late, and slid into a seat opposite Miss Rachel. He was still easy and unconcerned in manner, but he had added an air of subdued sorrow which he no doubt felt was expected in view of his brother's death.

He took a good drink of his wine as soon as it was poured. His eyes, on Miss Rachel, seemed to have a twinkle in them.

Butterworth suddenly looked about at all of them. "Sometime this evening I'd like to hold a council of war with you people. I've something to show you and some questions to ask. I'm hoping that some of you may have suggestions."

"I have a suggestion now," said Joe Dewel. "Let's have a party, a kind of wake for poor old Bart. I'll bring liquor, and . . ." His glance slid around the group. Only Miss Jennifer showed outrage, but she showed enough for everybody and the rest weren't looking enthusiastic. "Oh well, skip it. It seemed like a good idea at the time. Old Bart wouldn't want anybody grieving over him. He liked bright colors and bright people and a good time."

Butterworth went on as if there had been no interruption. "I'd like to see you folks in the little theater at about"—he glanced at a pocket watch—"nine-thirty. That's some time from now, but I've got a few things to do."

Sharon put up a hand to rub her temple. "Couldn't it wait until morning? I'm—I imagine everyone is tired."

"I'm sorry," said Butterworth without changing his tone. "This won't wait."

Dr. Page walked in. He made a neat, immaculate figure in evening clothes. He, too, thanked Sharon for her invitation to dinner. He explained that he was going on to another affair and wouldn't have had time to go home to change. In contrast with the business suits of the other men his clothes looked foppish, overelegant. Some of the effect was in the way he wore them. He was the expensive surgeon going out to make social conquests, the busy professional man taking time out for a bit of formal fun with his patients—the more successful ones of course. His humor was touched with a wise condescension. Miss Rachel decided she didn't care a lot for Dr. Page.

She must be in what Jennifer called her snap-turtle mood. After all Dr. Page might enjoy a change from white operating aprons and dull street clothes sometimes. And people expected doctors to be condescending; they were reassured then that the doctor knew more than they did. Which was necessary for even the simplest medicine to have proper effect.

Dinner went on without much further conversation.

It was later that Miss Rachel recalled that during the almond torte with wine sauce she had searched in her pocket for a handkerchief and had found none. She had found Mr. Braudryck's little match folders, but of course these were nothing to be shown at that moment.

She tugged Jennifer's skirt. Miss Jennifer regretfully turned her attention from the torte long enough to whisper that she didn't have a handkerchief either; she'd lost hers somewhere.

"In the boilers?" whispered Miss Rachel.

Miss Jennifer raised her voice. "I'll bring you down a handkerchief right after dinner, Rachel. Now be quiet."

Like a scolded child, Miss Rachel muttered: "Don't bother. I'll go get one myself."

Into the mind of someone at that table these words must have dropped like a stone into still, deep water.

Or perhaps they had floated through the open windows behind her. Outside the summer night sang with crickets. But anyone standing close to the wall should have heard hers and Jennifer's little exchange.

Coffee was served with the dessert at the table; there was no lingering after the meal. The sheriff and Dr. Page went off somewhere, perhaps for a hurried conference about medical matters relating to the murders. Mr. Braudryck mentioned some work he had lined up in Miriam's office. Rick just disappeared. Sharon went off wearily to rest until time for the meeting in the theater. Joe Dewel remained, to hover near the wine decanter.

"Bring me a handkerchief, too," said Jennifer mollifyingly. "I'm going into the kitchen and get the recipe for that torte."

Miss Rachel went up alone into the upper hall. Here was utter quiet. The air-conditioning unit made the hall a trifle chilly. Miss Rachel tried to turn the knob on her door. The door didn't move. It was locked. She hadn't locked it.

She stood quiet and put her ear to the panel and listened. Then she put her eye to the keyhole.

Her room seemed to be dark and empty. Perhaps the maid had carelessly locked the door after turning down the bed. Perhaps she herself had released some sort of spring catch without realizing it. Then she caught herself up abruptly; this was no time for muzzy thinking. There might be danger in that room, deadly danger. But why should the door be locked?

She thought it through. It would be presumed that she would, if careless, either go to get a key from one of the maids to let herself in or go in through Jennifer's room and the bath.

Those were careless ways and she would very likely be walking into a trap.

She retreated down the hall a way and watched the door, while a plan began to take form in her mind.

She went quickly and quietly downstairs and out through the door that led to the drive. In another two minutes she was approaching the barn. The white corral fence was ghostly against a smother of gloom. For a moment she was startled by a leafy scuttling sound from under a border of lantana. Then she heard her cat bound forth on hard little feet. She saw that there was a light inside the barn and she approached it cautiously.

From a high rafter hung a wire and at the end of the wire was hooked a lantern, shedding a yellow glow. Butterworth was taking precautions, or else he intended to work further out here tonight.

Several light pruning ladders lay against the wall. Miss Rachel chose one, hefted it, found it heavier than it looked. Since she couldn't carry it she would drag it. She was out in the corral, pulling the ladder briskly after her, when Miss Jennifer's voice spoke out of shadows.

"Crawling somewhere?" Miss Jennifer sounded waspish.

"My room is locked and I have a feeling there's something or somebody inside and I'm going to have a peep in through the window."

This seemed to stun Miss Jennifer into momentary silence.

Miss Rachel felt called on to defend her plan of action. "It's no worse than your antics this afternoon in those boilers. You weren't even worried about its being daylight either. When did you dig out those rhinestone garters of Aunt Lily's?"

Miss Jennifer said sputtering sounds.

"You've always disapproved of Mother's people because they were theatrical folk. Didn't you know the sort of show Aunt Lily was in when she wore those garters?"

Miss Jennifer hurriedly took up the other end of the ladder. "Be quiet, Rachel. We don't want to be discovered in this situation. Anyway, they were good garters and I needed a pair badly and waste is wicked. I meant to cut the rhinestones off but we came away in too much of a hurry. I did snip off a pair of big red satin hearts trimmed with ostrich feathers."

"Waste is wicked," murmured Miss Rachel.

"They're rather pretty and I'm going to make curtain tiebacks of them," snapped Miss Jennifer.

The thought of big red satin hearts holding back Jennifer's

starched white scrim made Miss Rachel smile. "They won't help your reputation."

"After the way *I've* lived," said Miss Jennifer righteously, "I can afford them."

"People are so unfair. Now if I——"

"And they'd be right," Miss Jennifer panted, going at a mad rate through a section of shrubbery. "And you wouldn't care."

The side of Miriam's house loomed up before them, pale under the starlight, its windows blank and shadowy.

"There," said Miss Rachel. "Those ought to be our windows."

They experimented with the ladder. Samantha came and stood close to watch them, a dark shining shape with eyes faintly green and gleaming. Miss Rachel went gingerly up the ladder and peered in through a pane. After a long time of peering she made out that this was Jennifer's room.

She came down and the ladder was moved. Some scraping sounds were made, and a little thump where the ladder came to rest.

"Be careful!" Miss Jennifer panted. "Don't let him catch you!"

The fear in Miss Jennifer's voice was contagious; Miss Rachel felt rattled by it. "Who?"

"Whoever's in your room, goose!"

"I didn't say for sure that anyone was in my room."

"Well, forever sakes . . ."

"But I'm going to have a look." She went up again, conscious of her heart's funny beating and a difficulty in getting her breath. She found the dark pane and put her nose to it.

There was a small light inside her room, a matchglow glimmer that showed her the fog her breath had made on the pane, the dark humped shapes of furniture, the white square where the bed stood. . . . She had a numb, icy sense of terror as she looked into the face on her pillow.

Mechanically she wiped away the frost of moisture on the window. On the bed matted curls shown with a yellow luster that dirt and leafmold did not quite conceal. The red lips curved in their vacant smile, the shallow eyes seemed mockingly to meet her own. From the crack above the temple ran the long, shining red stain which looked like fresh blood.

The little light, as before, was fixed to the doll's bosom. The scene had a waiting, evil, poisonous quality that made her shiver.

Miss Jennifer cried, "Don't shake the ladder so!"

"I'm—I'm coming down."

There was sudden, surreptitious movement inside the room, dark movement like the sweep of a hooded figure. The doll rose off the bed and flew toward her through the air. She had an instant's horrible closeup of the gleaming bloodlike stain, the porcelain smile fixed as in death, the tousled dirty hair, before she toppled off the ladder into an uncomfortably twiggy shrub below.

"Well, of all the clumsy——" murmured Miss Jennifer. Then she looked upward at the window and screamed.

The face wobbled against the black glass for a moment and then disappeared.

Miss Rachel, torn and scratched, got out of the shrub. The cat still sat watching; there was more than a hint in the faintly shining eyes that she thought her mistresses were crazy.

"Did you see it?" shrieked Miss Jennifer.

"Certainly I saw it. Do you think I made that back somersault for fun? The thing flew at me. Really, of course, someone ran at me holding the thing. . . . Ugh!"

Miss Jennifer's teeth were chattering audibly. "Why should anyone do such a trick, Rachel? Why pick on you, of all people?"

Miss Rachel untangled twigs and brushed away dust and bits of leaves. "Maybe I've been making a nuisance of myself."

"Rachel," breathed Miss Jennifer, "do you know who murdered Miriam and Mr. Dewel?"

Miss Rachel thoughtfully investigated a tear in her petticoat. "Yes, I believe I do. Of course there are some minor mysteries that have to be cleared up. Such as what you found in those boilers."

A clamlike silence ensued on Miss Jennifer's part. Miss Rachel sighed and went back to the foot of the ladder.

"Now what?" demanded Miss Jennifer.

"I'm going up to have another look."

"Who did it?"

"The murderer."

"Who is the murderer?"

Miss Rachel made strange, soft mumbling sounds.

"What's that?" demanded Miss Jennifer.

"That's the noise one clam makes to another clam," said Miss Rachel, going up rung by rung to put a very wary eye above the window sill.

"What do you see?"

"He or she or it has gone. The door's open and I can see through to the hall. Come on, let's go in."

"He might be waiting!"

"He's much too shrewd to be standing about in the hall. We'll check on everybody, incidentally, as we go in. You see if Mr. Braudryck's in the office and if Mr. Dewel's still with the wine bottle."

They separated. Miss Rachel found Butterworth in the little theater; he seemed to be examining some rolls of film. Dr. Page was at the front door, putting on driving gloves. He nodded to her absently.

Jennifer came racing up the hall, holding her skirts almost high enough to show Aunt Lucy's garters. She dragged Miss Rachel away with her, under the surprised eye of Dr. Page.

"Mr. Dewel's in Miriam's office," she panted. "He's robbing her wall safe!"

# CHAPTER FIFTEEN

Joe Dewel turned swiftly from the open wall safe. He no longer looked like a melting wax Santa Claus. He seemed hardened, thinned, assured. Even the liquor—and there had been plenty of that—could not bring back the old uncertain wobblings. He made no apology for having opened the safe.

"Come in, ladies. Do you mind pulling the door shut? Butterworth has such fuddy-duddy ideas."

"Sir——" began Miss Jennifer.

"Braudryck was here," went on Mr. Dewel, "but he stepped out suddenly. For a moment I thought that it was he who was coming in. I don't mind saying I'd rather see you ladies." He held a manila envelope in his hands, an envelope sealed with Miriam's big regal initial on dark blue wax. "I need witnesses, anyway, for this. I don't want to be accused later of stealing anything valuable."

Miss Jennifer drew another breath. "Sir, this is plain unvarnished robbery and the police——"

She stopped. Mr. Dewel had torn the end of the envelope and was peering into it. "All present and accounted for. No ma'am, the police wouldn't so much as lift a finger over these. Want to see?"

"I believe I know," said Miss Rachel. "Wisteria seeds?"

For an instant he showed surprise.

"I don't know the whole story. I'll have to admit that I peeked into the note Miriam sent to our house for you. I thought, when you saw them, the number seemed to disappoint you."

"Did I show it?" he asked.

"Rather strongly. I knew Miriam had sent you to persuade us to come here. She wanted my help because she was somewhat frightened about the things that were happening, the vicious mischief she couldn't quite solve. If I agreed to come you were to ask if there had been a note sent for you. I was to hand you the letter containing the wisteria seeds. It seemed obvious that the wisteria seeds were a reward for a job well done."

"The agreement was that all of the remaining seeds were to be sent," he said harshly. "She only sent three."

"She was probably already of half a mind to go on alone in her efforts to catch her tormentor—a decision she had made completely by the time we arrived. So she cheated on you. That was, unfortunately, like Miriam."

He let the wisteria seeds slide from the envelope to the glass-topped desk. They were dark and shining and big, perhaps eight or ten of them. "You're curious about the story behind them. Well, I might start by saying that I wasn't always Miriam's gutter pup. I used to own a grove of my own, nice oranges, some avocados. My wife was dead and I was trying to raise a son. Citrus prices weren't what they are now, but I made enough to run a decent home and keep a housekeeper, and to save up a bank account for the kid to use when he entered college. Of course I should have known when I was well off and left well enough alone—but I didn't. There were some stocks, oil stocks, that looked good—a new field near San Diego—and so I slapped a mortgage on my place and invested."

"I know what's coming next," said Miss Rachel uncomfortably.

"All at once, to my complete surprise, I found that I owed that money to Mrs. Hamilton. She'd bought my mortgage from the man I'd borrowed from, an old acquaintance who had promised to be easy on payments and interest collections. Well, she wasn't easy."

"And when she could she foreclosed on you."

He picked up a wisteria seed and dropped it on the desk with a small sharp *clink*. "Like that. I was out. Her men were at my place the day after the foreclosure, taking out trees that weren't producing, putting in young ones. She sent word that I could come up here and see her. She'd had influenza and was in bed, lying there like a queen, all fixed up under a lace spread that probably cost her about what my mortgage had. She told me I'd had bad luck, hoped I had other plans, said she was having the property evaluated for resale. All at once I woke up to the fact that under the law, by deficit on a tricky resale, she could take all my savings. I saw the kid's college career going up in smoke. Of course as a parent I hadn't been any great shakes maybe—but the boy's chance at college was something I'd wanted for a long time."

He poured out the last of the wine and stood regarding it with a half-bitter, half-amused glance.

"She had me over a barrel . . . and then she surprised me. She asked how much money I had. I didn't have a cent with me. I had a couple of dozen wisteria seeds that one of her gardeners had given me. I laid them on the bed, and I was mad all the way through."

He tossed the wine off at a gulp.

"She said in a kind of sly way that sometimes she needed a handy man for errands—confidential errands. If I wanted the job I could keep the money I'd saved for the boy to go to college. She'd furnish me a house and food and a little spending money. For the rest, in payment for her generosity, I'd have to earn back these wisteria seeds."

"For every job I suppose you'd get one or two," said Miss Rachel. "She loved to have people dangling and miserable. I'm glad that Sharon's father wouldn't dangle. By the way, did Ray Hamilton know of this deal you made with her?"

"He knew she took the land and that I stayed on afterward like a tramp waiting for a handout. I don't know what he thought. He never asked questions about it."

Feet sounded out in the hallway. Joe Dewel seemed lost in bitter memories, looking down at the little heap of seeds.

Miss Rachel went close and scooped up the seeds and put them back into the envelope. "Put these in your pocket. Close the safe. Plant your seeds in a sunny warm spot and some future springtime they'll repay you."

He took them absently. "I guess I'm a heel to involve you ladies in this mess. If I hadn't gone up to persuade you to come here——"

"Rachel would never have forgiven you," snapped Jennifer. "Those seeds had her fairly drooling."

"Strange the way Miriam changed her mind about consulting you," Dewel went on. "She wanted you to help her. She said you had a nose like a ferret. Oh, figuratively, of course."

"Figuratively in other people's business," said Miss Jennifer.

"Then she cooled all at once, before we got back here."

"I think she had found out the identity of the mischief-maker," said Miss Rachel.

A place twitched in his loose jaw. "Then who . . . ?"

Sheriff Butterworth pounded the door panel, then pushed the door open. "Here you are. Come along, please. We want everybody in the theater for some look at a film."

"You got a good double feature?" asked Mr. Dewel.

"Just so-so," said Butterworth.

In the theater, under shaded bluish lights, sat a group of waiting people. Mr. Braudryck looked drowsy. Sharon was straight and pale and enormous-eyed. Rick seemed made of stone. Another figure, a woman wearing a shabby gray coat and a close-fitting gray hat, sat alone and seemed out of place. The face came up and reddened eyes studied their entrance. It was Mrs. Krythe. She gave a misty nod in their direction, brushed her cheeks with a damp handkerchief, and straightened the gray hat on the fuzzy, faded hair. It struck Miss Rachel that Mrs. Krythe might once have had a sort of fragile, wildrose beauty, the kind of white-and-pink bloom that shrivels at the first touch of bitter living. Some little trace of loveliness remained, a shadow of what had been, and Miss Rachel recalled the strange talk of the cook's about a romance between Mrs. Krythe and Checkers.

Mrs. Krythe made a picture of misery. Miss Rachel went to sit by her, to touch her arm in a quiet offer of friendliness.

Mrs. Krythe looked at her for a moment, then let forth a burst of hoarsely whispered words. "Jerry wouldn't have done it. His being there doesn't convict him of anything. And he wasn't stealing oranges either. Old Mr. Boggs offered him a load of culls for the taking."

Miss Rachel recalled that there had been oranges in the truck when Jerry Krythe rattled by on the road. She surmised, also, that in this grove country an orange thief would have the same standing as a horse thief on the range.

"I'm sure no one is accusing him of stealing," she said to Mrs. Krythe.

"They're getting ready to accuse him of something. Why call me up here like this otherwise?" She stopped to choke on a sob. "He—he was taking a short cut below the old Hamilton place when Sharon called him. Why couldn't she have gone on her own errand?"

"Did he take the message to Butterworth about Dewel's murder?"

"When Sharon told him what had happened he ran away. He's hiding somewhere. . . . I can't blame him. He's been in a little trouble, everyone's against him. . . ."

"No, I'm sure that isn't true!"

She truly wanted to comfort Mrs. Krythe but the woman's whining pessimism got on her nerves. The damp handkerchief fluttered with Mrs. Krythe's agitated gestures.

"I'm only a widow . . . no influence . . . I haven't the money . . ."

"I'm sure that a little light shed on the subject will clear Jerry immediately," said Miss Rachel.

Mrs. Krythe seemed to sit suddenly still. Her head was bent and the line of her neck was tensed and startled.

After a moment she raised her eyes. Some expression Miss Rachel could not analyze flickered in her eyes and was gone.

At the rear of the room was an enclosed booth containing large projection machines and sound equipment. Butterworth, however, had brought out from a closet and set up the smaller machine used for screening home movies. He had two reels of film on the small table beside him. One of his deputies was stationed at the light switch.

"Okey, lights out," said Butterworth.

The room went dark. Curtains drew slowly aside at the front of the theater and a white light beamed out to settle on a screen.

Butterworth let the film begin without comment.

Miss Rachel found herself looking at an outdoor scene, on the floor of what seemed to be a rather wild little canyon. Two horses cropped desultorily at the dried grass. A blanket was spread on the sandy creek bed, now dry, under a dwarfed tree, and in the half shade sat Miriam. She wore severely tailored green jodhpurs, a soft gray sweater, a gray scarf on her head. She turned with a slow, almost theatrical precision toward the camera and the film caught the high, haughty look which had been habitual with her.

"My father took this," said Sharon.

"Uh-huh," agreed Butterworth. "We guessed that."

Suddenly the camera shifted, showed the approach to the canyon and a figure on a horse coming at a swift trot. The figure came closer, rounded a clump of manzanita, and there was Sharon—the Sharon of six or seven years ago with the straight figure and windblown hair of the teens. There was a hopeful, happy look on her face. She waved at the camera and pulled her horse to a stop.

At this point Miriam must have spoken. The girl in the picture jerked about to look in the direction of the tree and the spread blanket. For a moment she seemed to listen. The happy look went away. She turned her horse, touched his flank with her heel, and went off the way she had come.

Now the camera turned back with a furious haste to center upon Miriam. For an instant Miss Rachel had the strange feeling that it was she who had turned it. She thought: Take the spotlight then. Keep it. Send the child away and center everyone's attention on yourself.

Time seemed to stretch out with an eerie, angry tightness like that of an overkeyed fiddle string. The film whirred. There was just Miriam sitting strange and still, looking into the camera as if it fascinated her.

Joe Dewel said loudly: "Keep right on looking at the camera, baby. Now you've got what you wanted. Now Ray isn't noticing his kid."

Mr. Braudryck said, "Keep a civil tongue, Dewel. Mrs. Hamilton's dead, you know."

"Nuts to you," said Mr. Dewel.

Sharon made a soft sound like crying in the dark.

At the end Miriam raised her hand as if to say, "Stop!"

Then the film ended and the deputy switched on the lights.

Miss Rachel looked about at the others. Mr. Braudryck stared behind him at Mr. Dewel with a touch of anger. Mr. Dewel sneered. Rick was bent forward, frowning. Sharon had sunk into her chair and was resting her head against the chair back. Her eyes were shut and tears glittered on her cheeks. Mrs. Krythe seemed faintly puzzled. Butterworth seemed engrossed in his work with the machine.

All at once the lights went out again and the white beam settled on the screen.

Now the scene was a familiar one, that of the pool below Miriam's house. Sunlight lay in a yellow dazzle on the water, through which Rick's head came up like a seal's. It was a much younger Rick. He had in the picture the leggy, freckled look Miss Rachel recalled. He made a splashy maneuver in the water, then crawled out upon the sun deck.

The camera moved jerkily to the other end of the pool.

"I remember this," said Rick. "It was Sharon's birthday, her first birthday after Miriam and Ray were married. Miriam took these pictures." He added after a moment: "She didn't often take pictures of other people."

At the other end of the pool Ray Hamilton sat in a deck chair with Sharon at his knee. In Sharon's arms was a doll.

Seeing the fixed smile, the wide shallow blue eyes, Miss Rachel drew a sharp breath. It was a big doll, a beautiful doll. Its long gown was of soft pink silk. Little high-heeled slippers covered its feet. A gold chain winked on its throat.

The film stopped with the doll and Sharon and Sharon's father frozen there on the screen. Sharon's hand was stretched out to smooth a yellow curl. Ray Hamilton wore his easygoing, friendly smile.

Butterworth spoke harshly. "Mrs. Krythe, I want you to look carefully at the doll in this picture. Have you seen it before?"

The gulping noise made by Mrs. Krythe was clearly audible in the dark. "Y-yes, I believe I have."

"When?"

"A long time ago. Years ago."

"Under what circumstances?"

"Mr. Hamilton brought it to my shop. I'd just opened the ship, and I'd been doing dressmaking on order. I hadn't stocked my notions yet, I remember. It was just after the time Mrs. Hamilton began to make trouble for us. Dave and I needed money."

"About the doll," said Butterworth.

"Yes. Well, Mr. Hamilton brought the doll in a big cardboard box. The doll was in a dreadful shape, dirty and stained and molded. He said that it had been broken and that the person who had broken it had buried it to keep from admitting the truth. I think it had been buried, right enough. It looked it. Mr. Hamilton explained that it was a valuable doll, very old, and that he wanted it fixed up again for his daughter."

"And you repaired it?"

"No. You see, I couldn't do that. I could make clothes and perhaps clean it up a little. But the china head was cracked and the wig was just completely ruined. I told him he might try a doll repair shop in the city. He said for me to go ahead and take measurements and make a new set of clothes and that he'd have the doll fixed somewhere else."

"And you made the clothes as he asked you to?"

"I made them but he didn't ever come after them. He went off all of a sudden to Europe to paint pictures of the war."

"And what about the doll?"

"I don't know what he did with that. Honest I don't."

"Hey!" said Joe Dewel suddenly. "I know. I know what he did with it!"

Sharon's voice cried, "No! Don't say it! It's not true!"

The lights came on, flooding the scene with a bluish glow. Sharon was standing, gripping the back of the chair in front of her.

"Go on," said Butterworth ominously.

"Well, maybe I'm wrong then," said Joe Dewel reluctantly, "but Bart and I always thought Ray took that doll with him to France."

# CHAPTER SIXTEEN

A GREAT many facts became clear to Miss Rachel in that next moment. She had thought, for instance, that Sharon had been trying to protect Rick; and she had been wrong. Sharon had been trying to protect her father.

The doll had come back. Sharon thought that her father had come back too.

"He took it with him to France because he thought some of those Frenchies might do a better job of fixing it up," Joe Dewel said. "I remember hearing him tell Bart about it the night before he left. He was mad clear through. He knew Miriam had destroyed the doll in one of her rages."

Butterworth's mouth was like a trap. "Why haven't you mentioned all this before?"

"Why should I? Nobody asked me." Dewel glanced about as if puzzled.

This was true. Mr. Dewel hadn't been around at the time she and Jennifer had told of the doll's appearance. Even Butterworth did not know of the last appearance.

"I've told you your brother was murdered by a peculiar weapon," said Butterworth. "Well, a part of that weapon was the arm and hand off this doll. A huge needle like those used in her work by Mrs. Krythe——"

Mrs. Krythe made a shuddering sound.

"—was used as a blade, driven deep into the brain at the base of the skull."

Dewel's face twitched. There was a sudden frost of sweat across his upper lip.

"The handle of this weapon, the thing that enabled the killer to drive it home, was the hand of the doll."

"But *that* doll," said Dewel stumblingly, "went off to Paris with Ray. He might even have had it with him in that hell at Dunkirk. A lot of queer things happen in the war of course. Maybe somebody found the doll afterward and sent it back. Or . . . or maybe even . . ." His glance shifted to Sharon, flickered quickly away.

Sharon was stricken, bloodless, voiceless.

"No," said Butterworth, "Ray Hamilton didn't come back. That's one thing we're really sure of. Ray Hamilton is dead and he's buried in England. He was wounded at Dunkirk, got in with a last load of troops and died in some little launch out in the Channel. They took him on across. Did you think I wouldn't already have wired the War Department and *Day's Digest?* I had to plug that loophole right at the beginning."

Sharon didn't move. Her eyes filled slowly with tears. Some frantic, half-formed hope, mixed with as frantic a fear, was dying in her face.

She had had the hope, common to unnumbered others who had lost someone they loved in the war, that through some accident or imprisonment her father might still be alive. She had thought he might have come back to even a grisly score with

Miriam. The meaning of the remarks Bart Dewel had made on the terrace was clear now.

Bart Dewel and Sharon had both known of the anger Ray had felt over the destruction of the doll. Ray must have made some threat of reprisal. Bart Dewel had thought to use Miriam's murder to further his own ends. He had hinted, fostered, increased the growing thought Sharon had had that her father might have returned.

Miss Rachel came out of her abstraction to realize that Jennifer was relating the story of the doll's appearance that evening. Mercifully Jennifer left out the details of the topple into the shrubbery. She gave a vivid and accurate description of the doll.

Butterworth listened in an angry silence.

The question of why the doll's hand should have been used as part of the weapon returned to haunt her. She was deep in thought when she realized suddenly that everyone's eyes were on her as though she were expected to say something.

"Motive," said Butterworth in a tone of repeating something for a person slightly deaf. "Why would anyone want to scare you with this mumbo-jumbo?"

"There's a kind of pattern, an alikeness, about all of this if I can just figure it out," she said slowly. "Of course the reason the doll was used to torment Miriam was because it represented something she was ashamed of, something she wanted to keep secret. Even her imperious, ruthless mind would hate to acknowledge the uncontrolled rage which had caused her to trample and damage the doll. Then this destruction of the prize-winning fuchsias seems to have been part of the campaign. Lying in wait in my room in an attempt to terrify me was probably just trying to get rid of a nosy nuisance."

Miss Jennifer said acidly, "I never dreamed you'd admit it."

"I didn't say that I *was* a nosy nuisance," Miss Rachel corrected, "I meant that they think I'm one. Of course I do go right on thinking. All the time. I keep wondering what Miriam might have been about to do, or might have just done, to invite all this active hatred."

The little theater was quiet. The bluish light shone on the faces of the others, on Sharon's weariness and Rick's reserve, on Joe Dewel's alcoholic composure, on Mr. Braudryck's sly humor.

"I know what Miriam was about to do," said Mr. Braudryck.

Miss Rachel could have bitten her tongue. She'd invited this.

"Miriam was going to liquidate the Flanders estate," said Braudryck. "Rick was going to wake up someday soon without a dime. In fact he'd have been in debt."

A sudden look of cunning, of victory, came over the sheriff.

"I knew what was coming," said Rick expressionlessly. "I'm not a complete fool. Miriam was in a rage at Sharon and me. Sharon's father hadn't left anything Miriam could take from her. My dad left bank accounts and I knew that Miriam's first idea of revenge for these fancied wrongs would be to raid those accounts. I even knew how she'd do it. The methods open to her were right up Miriam's alley—doctored books and fake sales and a touch of discreet bribery."

"Put a little more heat into your voice, Rick," said Braudryck. "You're too unconcerned. You don't act natural."

"You come outside and I'll act natural," Rick promised.

"Here, here," said Butterworth. "Rick, what were your plans for self-protection?"

"I intended to let Miriam get a way into her dirty work, do some lying and have the books halfway juggled, and then try to pick a time when she'd be unprepared and descend on her with a court injunction and the best accountants I could find."

"Sounds pretty good," Butterworth grunted.

"Killing her was so much simpler," sneered Mr. Braudryck. Then, as Rick rose ominously, he added: "For somebody of course."

"Wait a minute," cried Miss Rachel. "Rick, you'll swear you weren't at the bottom of this mischief?"

Rick looked at her patiently. "If it helps . . . I'll swear I didn't do any of it."

Miss Rachel went on quickly. "My theory's been that Miriam had finally discovered the identity of the real culprit—that's why she didn't ask my help, that's why she was murdered. Then—and now I'm accepting Rick's word that he wasn't guilty—she shouldn't have been discussing with Mr. Braudryck this business of ruining Rick. Don't you see, it would have been *someone else* she'd have been after by then?"

All eyes had turned upon Braudryck. He remained silent and the reddish flush brought on by his afternoon drinking slowly went away.

Butterworth said grimly, "But she *was* still after Rick. Wasn't she, Braudryck?"

"Well. . ." Mr. Braudryck seemed to want time to think. "She had acted peculiarly, you know. Of course she hadn't mentioned any action except the one against Rick. But she went away inside very suddenly, without explanation."

"You told us at the time she'd gone in for a wrap," Miss Rachel reminded him. "And you can't straddle that fence forever. You've either got to say that she still suspected Rick alone and was planning to loot his father's estate in revenge or that the conversation was about some other subject entirely."

The look he gave her was full of a kind of remote hatred, as though she were a troublesome bug buzzing about while he tried to think.

"It was about Rick," he said suddenly. "Maybe Rick wasn't at the bottom of the mischief but she thought he was and she intended to take action."

Butterworth waved the deputy away from the light switch. "Come here and put away this stuff," he said. "Rick, I guess you know what's coming next."

"I guess I do," said Rick.

Butterworth took out a pair of handcuffs and they clanked together loudly in the sudden quiet. Mrs. Krythe said, "Oh no!" Rick stood up and Sharon touched his hand softly with her own.

Mrs. Krythe stammered, "Are you arresting him for killing Bart Dewel, too, Sheriff? Because if you are, maybe you'd better wait. Jerry was getting the load of culls near the Hamilton place and maybe he saw something. . . ."

As if to remind them all the more clearly of Jerry, there came the far-off, popping sound of a motor. Perhaps the old motor in Jerry's little truck. Was Jerry out there, riding around in the dark, afraid to come forward with what he knew?

"I'm only taking Rick in for questioning," said Butterworth shortly. "If he'll go quietly I won't even use these handcuffs. Some of these young fellows who've been away in the Army think they're pretty tough. I don't want any trouble."

"I'll come quietly," said Rick. "Good-by for now, Sharon. Don't worry about me. Thanks, Miss Rachel, for all you've tried to do."

"I've just started," said Miss Rachel. "Sheriff, are you going to try to prove that Rick was the one guilty of the mischief?"

"I'm going to leave that damned doll and the fuchsias absolutely alone, except as incidental to Miriam's motive in going after Rick. She thought Rick did it. We can prove that. She was planning a dirty campaign to make Rick a pauper. I guess that's all we'll need to start on."

"Do you mind if I go on, on that particular line?"

"Hop to it."

"Will you arrest the person guilty if I can prove guilt?"

Caution flickered in Butterworth's steel-colored eyes. "Well, now, I don't quite know on what charge I'd hold him—providing, of course, there's proof. Malicious mischief, maybe, though it seems more like a prank."

"The destruction of Miriam's prize-winning fuchsias was a clear damage to something which had cost money," Miss Rachel pointed out.

The word "money" had the proper effect. "That's true. We'll hold the person on malicious mischief then."

"And for questioning in regard to the murders?" she prodded.

He resented being prodded. His face expressed his desire that she shut up. "Well, if there's evidence of a connection."

"Of course there's a connection," Miss Rachel snapped. "The whole thing is a mass of connection. Miriam was being driven to fury by the nocturnal visions of that horrible doll and the vicious damage to her flowers. She was murdered behind the door to the lath house, where the fuchsias grew. Bart Dewel was murdered with a weapon made partly out of the hand of the doll." She stopped suddenly, wrinkled her nose and forehead in a concentration of racing thought.

"You look exactly like a white rabbit smelling a lettuce leaf," said Miss Jennifer drolly.

"I almost had it," said Miss Rachel. "I almost had *it.*"

"What?" asked Miss Jennifer scornfully.

"The—the pattern, the alikeness . . ."

"Well," said Butterworth, "you just got through saying the whole thing was connected——"

"No, deeper than that—and hooked onto some other fact I keep feeling is skipping around my mind like a moth."

Butterworth's air of being a businessman suddenly evaporated. He was, after all, a cop. "Come on, Rick. I'll wait while you get some stuff together. We can't stay here gabbing all night. Miss Murdock, if you find out something important give me a ring. I agree with you that certain elements of the mischief seemed to be woven into the murders. Maybe it's a false clue, trying to involve someone else. Anyway, call me if you find out anything definite."

"Definite!" mimicked Miss Rachel in Jennifer's room. "He wants something definite! Some definite lie of Mr. Braudryck's, I suppose."

"Well, after all, he can't wait until your thoughts quit flitting around like moths. The police have to be sensible and hardheaded."

"While we're talking of sensible people—what were you doing in those boilers?"

Miss Jennifer, seated gingerly on the edge of the purple-and-white bed, maintained an obdurate silence.

"Did you poke about up there long? Were you there, say, at about one o'clock?"

Miss Jennifer cautiously asked, "Why?"

"Well, being up on the hill and overlooking the village, you might have been able to say whether Mrs. Krythe was at home while Bart Dewel was being murdered."

"I saw no sign of Mrs. Krythe. That doesn't prove anything."

"Do you have any further business in those boilers?"

More silence. Then, since curiosity was a torment: "Why?"

"Because I'm going down to try to have a look at Mrs. Krythe's doll-repair business and I'd like company. You can explore the boilers while I break into Mrs. Krythe's shop."

"In broad daylight?"

"It's almost midnight, goose."

"You—you mean——"

"Yes, I mean."

"Rachel, don't! You'll be caught and put into jail. It's open burglary!"

"It isn't open burglary until they catch me. Are you coming?"

"Rachel, I'll admit something. There wasn't a thing in those boilers but a lot of spider webs and dirt and a dead mouse."

"Why were you in there?"

The clamlike silence returned.

"Oh well, it probably isn't important. Are you coming with me now?"

"Rachel, this sort of thing will eventually get you into serious trouble. As I said when you began by opening that letter to Mr. Dewel, it's best to stick to the law."

"Mrs. Krythe's got something on her mind. A feeling of guilt perhaps? She didn't want them to take Rick away, she tried to delay them by saying Jerry might know something. Maybe if we go down to the shop we'll run into Jerry."

"We'll much more likely run into Sheriff Butterworth."

"He is tiresome that way, isn't he? Always lurking about."

"Rachel, where are you going now?"

"I'm going into my room for a coat and a scarf for my head. I brought a black scarf in case I needed to run about at night. My hair's unfortunately so white. Aren't you coming?"

"I—I don't know."

"The theater was stuffy. We need air."

"Jails are stuffy, too, Rachel. I know. I was in one once."*

Since Miss Jennifer's having been in jail was Miss Rachel's fault, this had a slightly chastening effect. Miss Rachel went after her wraps at a discreet walk instead of a trot. When she came back Jennifer was wearing a knitted cape, the black toque, and had just snapped the last fastener on a pair of black cotton gloves.

She held out a brown pair to Miss Rachel.

"You astonish me sometimes. How did you happen to think of gloves, Jennifer?"

"Fingerprints," said Miss Jennifer grimly. "Remember, mine are already on file."

They went out, discovering to their annoyance that their cat had followed and was playing at mouse catching under the shrubbery. She rattled the dried leaves and growled playfully and made ballet leaps out upon the drive. Miss Jennifer wanted to go back.

"We'll go down past the barn and find the trail Joe Dewel must have taken this morning, after he'd eavesdropped on the sheriff and Dr. Page." She flicked a brief beam from Jennifer's flashlight out across the gravel. Presently, ahead, there shone out the faint glow of the lantern left burning in the barn. "It's probably a short cut to the village, or it joins the path I followed this afternoon."

The door of the barn yawned open, full of yellow light. They glanced in.

The lantern still hung by its long wire from the rafters.

Hung to it by a shred of dirty rope was the doll.

---

* *The Cat Wears a Noose*, American Mystery Classics, 2024

# CHAPTER SEVENTEEN

THE DOLL swung slowly in circles as though someone had just hung it in place and hurried away. Around and around it turned at the end of the scrap of rope, one arm a ragged stump from which still drifted a grain or two of sawdust, the eyes blue and staring, the cracked head still seeming to bleed. At the waist, pinned into the half-rotted cloth of the gown, was a pencil-sized flashlight pointed upward. This explained the illumination, the matchlike glow that had seemed to rise, to move with the doll.

"Oh, horrible, horrible!" gasped Miss Jennifer.

But Miss Rachel went in to touch the doll softly, to look into its face. "Now it can be beautiful again, the way it was meant to be. Now it doesn't have to be shown at night, evilly, frightening people. A little child's doll shouldn't be used so. It makes me quiver with anger."

"We'd better quiver out of here," said Miss Jennifer.

"There isn't any hurry now. The doll was an embarrassment, once Rick was under arrest. It might be traced to the real mischief-maker and Rick might thus be cleared. There won't be any mumbo-jumbo while Rick is gone. He's supposed to be the guilty one."

"But this doll being here—Rick couldn't have done this."

"We believe that he couldn't, but what proof have we? It's possible, I suppose, for him to have slipped out here just before the meeting in the theater."

She put up a finger tip to scratch thoughtfully at the bulging red stain on the doll's forehead. Jennifer asked, "What's that stuff?"

"It's lipstick, I think. It's been melted and poured on."

"Must we stand about?" Jennifer complained. "I'm nervous."

"You stay here. I'm going back to the house to call Butterworth on the telephone. I'm going to tell him about finding the doll."

"He said he wouldn't have anything to do with it."

"I'll tell him there are clues." Miss Rachel took out the two little match folders, crushed one into a crack in the floor under the doll and dropped the second in the shadows near the door. "No, this second one's too obvious." She picked it up again. "Maybe I shouldn't mention anything about clues. He might get suspicious. What do you think, Jennifer?"

"If those are what I think they are, Rachel, your conscience shouldn't let you sleep nights."

"I haven't much conscience when it comes to Mr. Braudryck," Miss Rachel admitted. "Wait for me. I'll be right back."

Ten minutes later they were on a pathway that wound, in devious and untended ways, down the hill toward the village. The night had little wind and was warm and full of the scent of orange blossoms. The sky wore the velvety black look of deep midnight.

In the village no lights shone except two lonely street lamps at either end of the business block.

"Skulk, Jennifer. We're going to duck down the alleyway behind this bar. You're marching along as though you were going to church."

"Would that I were!" snapped Miss Jennifer.

With a quick look around Miss Rachel led the way down the weedy space, now black as pitch, and into the cleared area behind the row of stores.

After some scrambling through waste boxes, piled bottles, and other odds and ends Miss Rachel whispered, "This should be the back of Mrs. Krythe's store. Is there room back here for living quarters?"

"Turn on the flashlight," whispered Jennifer. "If it *is* living quarters we can run."

The flashlight beam showed a shedlike addition to the body of the store. Miss Rachel ventured to the door and shone the light in through the pane. Inside were neatly stacked boxes, shelves with assorted goods, and a narrow table piled with yardage. A door led into the bigger room.

Miss Rachel rattled the knob experimentally, then made vain efforts with bent hairpins. "Well, we'll use a window. You go and try the ones on the other side of the building. If you find one open holler."

"Holler! Rachel, your grammar!"

"Never mind. This one right beside the door isn't fastened." The pane slid up under the pressure of her fingers. There wasn't any screen. She climbed through. "Isn't this the silliest thing, locking the door and then leaving a window right—*ouch!*"

Miss Jennifer jumped.

"A nail," moaned Miss Rachel, sucking her palm.

Footsteps sounded on the sidewalk: slow, ominous footsteps that seemed to boom at them out of the dark. Miss Rachel, inside the storeroom, clicked out the light.

The footsteps came inexorably closer.

They paused at last at what must be the entrance to the alleyway. Panting with fear, Miss Jennifer flung herself at the window and toppled through. There was a prolonged sound of ripping.

"Clever Mrs. Krythe," groaned Miss Rachel. "She's in the dressmaking business, so when she leaves a window open, she also leaves a big nail sticking——"

"Shhhh!" said Miss Jennifer with a sort of silent scream. "And don't move. Somebody's coming. *Here!*"

It was true. The slow, plodding, carefully placed footsteps were coming down the space between the buildings. Through the thin wall of Mrs. Krythe's storeroom they heard the *clunk, clunk, clunk,* with little cracklings of dead weeds and brief scatterings of gravel.

It occurred to Miss Rachel that there was something strange about those footsteps. The quality that had at first seemed like caution now resembled something else—like the blundering progress of someone blindfolded. Blindman's buff. *Blindman* . . .

"It's Checkers!" Miss Rachel whispered.

"My skirt and petticoats!" moaned Jennifer.

For a moment Miss Rachel thought that Jennifer had composed a new exclamation, something on the line of "my stars and garters," but a repetition of the moan, with deep emphasis, caused her to doubt. "What did you say?"

"Gone! Torn off! Ripped completely away by that horrid nail! If we should have to run, if I have to go near those street lamps . . . !"

The thought of Miss Jennifer twinkling through the night in Aunt Lily's rhinestone garters made Miss Rachel want to giggle cruelly. But she was coldly fascinated, too, by the heavy approach of the steps outside.

Checkers's voice, close to the door, said, "Jerry? Jerry, you here yet?"

There wasn't any answer except a crouching shiver from Miss Jennifer. Then the door creaked loudly and for a breathless moment Miss Rachel thought that he was coming in. Then there was a sigh and after a while pipe smoke drifted in through the window. Checkers had sat down on the step, his back against the door, to wait for Jerry.

Inside the dark little storeroom the silence grew long and eerie. Miss Rachel heard Jennifer's stirrings, then the inching progress she made across the floor.

"I'm cold," Jennifer whispered in her ear, "and half my clothes are still hanging up there on that nail."

"I'm trying to think."

"Then think about me. How can I go home, even in the dark, in just a waist and bloomers?"

"Shhh! Listen!"

Above the chattering of Miss Jennifer's teeth came the sound of more footsteps, light, not blundering, careless as only youth is careless. Checkers said, "Jerry?"

"Hi," said Jerry, sitting down and causing the step to creak. "Mother wanted me to meet you. I think it's better to keep out of sight. The cops'll put the whole mess off on me if they get the chance."

"Not now they won't. They've got Rick Flanders. They're going to pin it all on him."

"Oh."

The silence was more uncanny than the low-voiced, urgent conversation.

Checkers said at last, "It'll look better for you and it'll make your mother happier if you come forward and tell the truth."

"I'm afraid," Jerry said simply. "I don't think I got a square deal before, in that trouble about the old lady's hedge. Why should she have a hedge that dirtied my mother's washing?"

"That's all past, Jerry. You know, your mother would rather've gone on as things were than have you in trouble. That's how things are now, son. You've got to come out honestly and tell what you know."

There was more silence—a hint of stubbornness on Jerry's part perhaps. Then he said slowly, "I'd been down in the grove picking up a load of culls old man Boggs gave me. I was going to peddle them house to house in Santa Ana. I sacked the culls and had five sacks in the truck. Then, on my way to the truck with the last sack, I thought I'd cut across below the old Hamilton place——"

Checkers interrupted. "You've got to have an explanation for that when you talk to Butterworth. Why did you cut across with just that last load?"

"Well, I didn't have a sackful, if you've gotta know."

Checkers said seriously, "You can't tell Butterworth you were going to steal oranges, Jerry. You've got to have some other reason."

"Who'd care if I had stolen a few oranges? The woman who swiped all that land from other people was dead. They don't even know yet who all that property belongs to."

"I guess most of it belongs to Rick, poor fellow. Maybe that's one reason Butterworth's so sure he killed her." He drew a long, sucking breath through the pipe. The odor of the pipe tobacco, strong and spicy, drifted in to tickle Miss Rachel's nose. "Anyway, don't you tell Butterworth about wanting to get any more oranges. You just say you was tired and took a short cut."

The silence returned. The chattering of Miss Jennifer's teeth made a faint sound in the dark of the storeroom.

Finally Jerry, as if unwilling, said, "Maybe I ought to tell Butterworth what I found. You see, I think Bart Dewel must have been murdered *by a woman.*"

"What's that?"

"A woman." There was a rustling, rummaging sound as if Jerry were digging into a pocket. Then a match flared. "Look here. Look what I picked up on that short-cut trail."

Miss Rachel craned her neck so as to hear every least sound. She wished that she dared stick her head out and see what Jerry held.

"Three of them," said Jerry softly. "They're the kind that come in women's make-up kits. I know, because Mother had some kits like this in the store a while back."

The objects he held, whatever they were, clinked faintly as he handled them.

"But *three*," objected Checkers. "I don't get that part of it."

"Well, some women are awful particular how they look," said Jerry. "Mrs. Hamilton was. Miss Sharon is, in a way, though she wears black clothes all the time. I mean, even in those clothes she looks pretty. Of course Mother doesn't fix up. She wouldn't be carrying these things."

"How were they on the trail?" Checkers asked curiously. "Sort of dropped, like somebody'd do in a hurry?"

"Yeah. About twenty feet apart, I'd guess, just after you got into the trees."

"I don't see any meaning in it."

Jerry sounded uncomfortable. "No, I don't either. Except I'd judge the killer, or whoever was running away, was a woman."

"You make up a story and stick to it like glue," Checkers counseled, "because when Butterworth finds out you know something he's going to put you through the hoops. You stand up to him, son. Remember you'll be a big man in these parts someday. You'll keep your land, now Mrs. Hamilton's dead, and you might even be able to get damages out of the estate. You keep your chin up around Butterworth."

"Sure," said Jerry uneasily. "Sure I will."

"Well, we'd better be leaving. You staying home tonight?"

"No. I—I'm staying at a friend's house."

"Do what your mother wants. You won't regret it. And don't let Butterworth get you down. . . ."

They had risen from the step and were moving away.

Miss Rachel risked sticking her head from the window. All she saw was the black alleyway and two moving shadows against the faint light at its entrance, where the street lamp lit the sidewalk. There was a brief momentary wink of light from the slighter figure—Jerry's—as though a reflected beam had hit upon some bright surface. Miss Rachel's thoughts went back uncomfortably to the scene on the terrace, to Mrs. Krythe's humble exit, carrying her roll of chintz samples. There had been then a little flash, a fugitive brilliance . . . and it had been the needle which had killed Bart Dewel.

"They've gone, Rachel. Oh, my petticoats!" Miss Jennifer got up off the floor and loosened her voluminous skirts from the nail by the window. "Torn, riddled, hopeless!"

"No doubt Mrs. Krythe keeps a stock of safety pins for sale," Miss Rachel comforted her. "I'd give anything to know what Jerry Krythe found on the trail below the Hamilton place. It couldn't have been the trail I took or I'd have noticed. . . . He said the short-cut trail, didn't he, Jennifer?"

"I don't know. How can you worry over Jerry Krythe when here we stand in the act of burglarizing his mother's store?"

"I'll risk the flashlight." She turned the light around the room. "Not here, Jennifer, go in and pull down the front window shades while I rummage a bit, just in case."

"In case of safety pins?"

"No, I'd already forgotten them. I want Mrs. Krythe's records, if she keeps any. Her books where she lists credit work and so forth."

Miss Jennifer stumbled through the dark to the front windows while Miss Rachel searched vainly in the storeroom for any business account books.

"Come on in," said Jennifer in a shivery voice, "and get it over with. I keep expecting Sheriff Butterworth to pop up from behind the counter." She held her skirts about her with both hands.

By the light of the flash Miss Rachel explored a small, battered desk in a rear corner. If Mrs. Krythe could have been said to keep records, it was in an all-embracing manner. She kept everything. The desk was crammed with bills, receipts, sales records, credit jottings, work orders, and just plain junk.

While Miss Jennifer did frightened and rebellious sentry duty Miss Rachel sat at the desk and read. The profitable status of Mrs. Krythe's business must be in doubt even to its owner, for there was no consecutive arrangement of papers, no totaling of profit and loss, no accounting of money handled.

She came at last, and much to her own surprise, to the record concerning the doll's garments. The original order was dated more than five years before.

In Mrs. Krythe's scrabbling handwriting was jotted down:

*On order, for Mr. Ray Hamilton*
*One set of doll's garments*
*Gown*
*Hat*
*Underwear*
*Cape*
*Mittens*

There followed a list of measurements.

Below, in a larger, more masculine (and queerly uncertain) hand was written out:

*Paid in Full by Check. Ray Hamilton.*

And the date on this last notation was exactly *ten days ago!*

# CHAPTER EIGHTEEN

"Psssst!" hissed Miss Jennifer from the window. "Here's somebody, almost on the step! Oh, Rachel, turn off that flashlight!"

The light clicked off and in the dark they fled back to the storeroom and stood listening. A key scratched and rattled in the front-door lock. Then hinges yawned.

"Outside in a hurry!" commanded Miss Rachel. Jennifer hesitated, gripping her petticoats, and to speed things Miss Rachel went through first. Once on the ground, she found a wad of garments thrust at her.

"Hold these until I get through," panted Jennifer. There were scrabbling sounds on the window sill. Then the garments were snatched away. Dimly Miss Rachel made out that Jennifer was wrapping herself again in her clothes. She made breathless moaning sounds about safety pins.

"Wait here and listen!"

"Rachel, as I am! No, I'm going to the house. I'm cold and my knees are knocking together with fright and I'm——"

She choked and bit off what she was saying. A light had come on suddenly inside the storeroom. Mrs. Krythe stood in the middle of the floor and looked about as if on a hunt for something. She seemed angry and full of purpose. It was queer, Miss Rachel thought, how changed she was, how being angry had wiped out the fuzzy air of being humble and polite and fearful of doing wrong. Under the brim of her gray hat Mrs. Krythe's face was blazing, tense, alive.

Then she saw the open window and an odd sour half-smile twisted her lips. "If you're still out there watching, come back in. I won't hurt you."

Miss Jennifer tiptoed guiltily away in the dark. Miss Rachel waited in the perimeter of shadow, fascinated.

Mrs. Krythe folded her arms across her bosom. "So you aren't just a sneak and a thief. You're a coward, a chickenhearted coward, too."

Miss Rachel ventured out to where the light from the window shone on her. For a moment Mrs. Krythe showed surprise. Then contempt returned. "I'd have sworn it was Butterworth."

"Might I talk to you for a little while?" asked Miss Rachel.

"What's the matter? Didn't you find what you wanted to steal?"

"Oh yes, I found that," said Miss Rachel. She thrust out the hand which still held the order for the doll's clothes. Mrs. Krythe's eyes narrowed as she read it. Then she reached swiftly to snatch it away.

Miss Rachel, even more swiftly, had withdrawn her hand. The step which Mrs. Krythe had made in her direction took her from under the light. Her face was now in shadow. Miss Rachel could hear her hoarse, heavy breathing.

In a new voice, a throaty rough voice, Mrs. Krythe said, "The order is the same one I made out long ago when Ray Hamilton came to my store, bringing Sharon's doll. That last line, though, is something I'd never seen before. *It's a forgery.*" She put out a hand, slowly, compellingly. "The paper is mine. Give it to me."

"I haven't any intention of giving it to you. You know that." Miss Rachel moved away and in the shadows she gathered her skirts to a height Miss Jennifer would have gasped over. "This page is a part of Miriam's murder and of Bart Dewel's murder. It's evidence. If I give it to you, you'll burn it immediately."

Mrs. Krythe's pale eyes glittered. "Why should you think that?"

"You know why I think it. The notation on the bottom of this bill was to have clinched, tied up, completed the plot. Only . . . *Miriam was supposed to come searching for it.* Not me."

"Mrs. Hamilton wouldn't have come here," said Mrs. Krythe bitterly.

"Miriam Hamilton would have robbed your store at night with less conscience than she would have taken your lands by day. You knew that. Anyone who knew Miriam at all knew that she was utterly without scruples."

Mrs. Krythe shivered in the sudden grip of an emotion: anger or apprehension or fear.

"There was just one person Miriam ever fooled. There was one person she loved genuinely enough to wear a false front for—one person she would have given her world to go on deceiving."

Mrs. Krythe's mouth twisted again in its strange half-smile. "You're speaking of Mr. Hamilton."

Miss Rachel went on, "While Ray Hamilton was alive Miriam went about her land grabbing very cautiously. Some things she passed up entirely for fear the stories would get back to her husband, to the absent-minded artist who didn't know yet what she was."

Mrs. Krythe said in a steely tone, "Like taking my land while Dave was in the sanitarium?"

"Yes. She let that opportunity slip. Only, of course, with Ray Hamilton dead, Miriam's conscience was dead. She was gradually becoming more ruthless than ever. So how nice, if she could be frightened or persuaded into believing that Ray Hamilton was still alive."

"You think, then, that all this business with the doll—and this forgery on my order sheet—was meant to make her think that?" She reached the window sill suddenly in a kind of glide. "Don't go. I'm really interested. Stay and talk. . . ."

*Stay and be trapped.*

A figure had crept into the narrow alleyway from the street, a crouching, slow-moving shape that made no noise, that Miss Rachel suddenly saw for what it was in a burst of terror. Even being alert and on edge, even having her skirts and her legs ready for running, she was slow in getting away. She stumbled through darkness, away from the yellow square of the window. She wanted to call for Jennifer and knew that the sound of her voice would betray her whereabouts. She didn't dare use the flashlight. If only, she thought desperately, she had fixed more firmly in mind the exact way she and Jennifer had come from the other entry, the one beside the bar.

She ran into and fell over a beer barrel, scrambled up, and started a clatter among bottles. The dark was intense. It was like rushing through a maze, with false turns and traps at every step. In the long ago, in childhood, she recalled irrelevantly, she'd read a book about a boy who went into a maze to destroy a monster. He'd found his way out again by means of a string. Well, the monster in this case was behind her, a half-seen creeping shape.

All she needed to do was to scramble away fast enough; almost any direction would do.

How silly to be remembering an old tale while she fought and crawled her way through the hampering dark, a possible murderer behind her, every ounce of wits she possessed necessary to save her.

But her thoughts flew back yearningly, foolishly, to that piece of string the boy had had. . . .

*A piece of string!*

She stumbled out upon the sidewalk. She wanted to stop and think about the amazing connectedness, the completeness, of the crimes as she saw them now: all fitted together, hanging on that one other fact she already knew. Ahead the street lamp threw a yellow glow against the dark. She fled through the pool of light, on into the rising path that led up Miriam's hill.

Her side hurt from running, she'd cut her hand on some glass, and there was an ache in her throat from hard and heavy breathing.

She thought once that she caught the sound of a motor on the hill—whether climbing or descending, she couldn't tell; and knowing what she knew now she stopped breathlessly to listen. If it were Butterworth's car it wasn't important.

*If it were Braudryck's . . .*

She found the little shelter that overlooked the dark and silent village. The two street lamps were firefly gleams below, the business block shuttered, motionless. The breeze that touched her cheek was cold—as cold as the selfish greed that had crept through this valley. She shivered. The sun would rise again, the valley grow warm. Something more than night would have been cast away.

A sudden shaking of the honeysuckle hedge which surrounded the pergola made her whirl to face the entry. For a moment there was nothing but the dark; no crouched form, no creeping monster. Then from under deep shadow two faintly green and shining eyes blinked at her.

She had forgotten Samantha. Somewhere on their journey to the village she and Jennifer had lost the cat. She bent down, called comfortingly, "Here, kitty." Samantha came, was warm and silky under her hand, nipped gently at the fingers which stroked her ears.

Miss Rachel finished the climb and came out of the grove beside Miriam's pool which shimmered faintly under the starshine. Above, the terrace was dark and the towering house beyond it showed only a dim light here and there. The breeze which swept the hilltop had a fresh smell of salt water in it. Out beyond the long slope of the rich rolling land the Pacific thundered. Miss Rachel took a deep breath before she went into the dim quiet of the hall.

In the bathroom Miss Jennifer sat wrapped in a blanket on the edge of the tub. Her feet were planted solidly in ten inches of steaming water. When she saw Miss Rachel peering in at her she coughed dramatically.

"I've been very stupid," said Miss Rachel humbly.

The cat reached up, put forepaws on the tub's broad edge, and stared curiously in at Miss Jennifer's feet.

"Like you," said Miss Jennifer crossly, "always making a mystery out of nothing. They're feet." She held a set of reddened toes out to the cat and Samantha sniffed at them solemnly.

"The inquiring mind can't help inquiring," defended Miss Rachel. "But as I say, mine's been slow and foolish."

"And larcenous," added Miss Jennifer. "Let me see that paper you took from Mrs. Krythe's desk."

From her pocket Miss Rachel produced the paper. "She was quick to say that it was forgery. She didn't say whose. She looked as though she knew."

"I've suspected that woman from the beginning. She's sneaked and spied and been thoroughly underhanded, and then when she thought someone was watching she was too nice for words. Mealymouthed."

"She learned deceit in a hard school," Miss Rachel said. "She wanted to keep on some sort of terms with Miriam. She'd have a chance that way to know a little of what was going on, perhaps even get a hint as to when Miriam meant to strip her finally of all she owned. So we can't be too harsh in judgment."

"What are you going to do with that sheet of paper?"

"I'd like Sharon to see it, since this last line is supposed to be her father's writing."

"Sharon's sleeping. I peeped in a little while ago to ask if she had any cold remedies. The room was dark."

Miss Rachel's white brows feathered together in a frown. "I think that this is important enough to wake her." She went into her room and left her wraps and the flashlight. With Samantha following she went out into the hall.

Sharon's room was dark and quiet. Curtains moved softly at the windows, white and filmy against the black pane. The dim glow from the hall, however, showed Sharon across the room in a chair, looking out into the night.

"Sharon?"

"Oh. Hello. I'm over here. Did you look in earlier?"

"No, that was Jennifer."

"I was lying still trying to count sheep. Now I've given it up. Come in. Would you like a light?"

"Perhaps we'll need a little one." Miss Rachel touched the switch of a small table lamp near the door and crossed to where Sharon sat. She remembered this room, the plain narrow bed, the simple furnishings Sharon had brought from her father's house. She sat down in a chair that faced Sharon's.

"I've been thinking about Rick," said Sharon quietly, "and remembering how good and how understanding he's been. I—I've come to realize a good many truths about myself too. I know that the feeling I have for Rick isn't just the result of growing up together, of being used to him, of being most of the time jointly on the defensive against Miriam. I'd love Rick if I'd never seen him before."

Sharon's eyes had lost their long-ago questioning look. They were wise, awakened, saddened.

"I can see, too, how foolishly I've acted about Dad's death. Rick tried to make me give it up—the black clothes, the constant show of mourning—and I accused him of not understanding. Now I know that I wasn't really displaying a grief for Dad. The sorrow I felt over his death was too deep, too sincere for external things. I was just trying to punish Miriam, to keep reminding her of Dad's dying." She looked frankly into Miss Rachel's eyes. "It isn't fun, seeing yourself and your motives clearly."

"We all have what I suppose might be called psychological deeps," said Miss Rachel, "in which the swimming is pretty chilly."

"I—I haven't been exactly honest with you either. I know you meant to help, I even saw at last how entirely you were on Rick's side. I could have told you about finding the needle in my typewriter case. After Bart Dewel left the terrace, when I opened the lid . . ."

Miss Rachel recalled Sharon's odd absorption with something inside the case.

"Apparently it had fallen from the table the evening before and lodged in the case. The catch is defective and doesn't close tightly. In taking the typewriter out, I'd missed seeing it."

"What did you do with that needle?"

"I . . ." Sharon drew a long breath. "It seems incredible, but I took that needle with me when I went to meet Bart Dewel at the studio. I'd read—silly stories where the heroine stuck an annoyer with a hatpin. . . ." She shuddered deeply, drew her robe tight across her shoulders. "He was a very obnoxious man but he didn't deserve—that."

"Butterworth says that Bart Dewel had been in the process of writing something—that he had a pen under his hand and that a sheet of paper had slid to the floor."

"I don't know anything about those things."

"Will you tell me about your first visit, the one Rick broke in upon?"

She nodded. "I went early but Bart was earlier. He made a few remarks about the doll, about how one might think Dad hadn't died at Dunkirk but might have been imprisoned, had amnesia, and things like that. He must have seen how terrified I was."

"And the needle?"

"I guess I dropped it."

"Did you pass anyone—closely—on your way here?"

"I don't think so. No, wait. Checkers." She frowned, puckering her smooth brow. "I asked him if he'd seen you."

"How close were you to Checkers?"

"At least fifteen feet away. He doesn't see well, you know. He must have recognized my voice. I remember asking if he'd seen you about. He said he'd try to find you."

It was true, Miss Rachel recalled, that while she had been exploring the barn, finding the place behind the door where Miriam had been killed, Checkers had come in, calling her name.

It all fitted perfectly now. There no longer was any shred of doubt. There remained a simple test, an official search of Braudryck's car, then climax.

She suddenly hated the part that she must play.

# CHAPTER NINETEEN

It almost never rains in California in early September. The mornings are often heavy with fog, so heavy that earth and grass is soaked and trees drip huge spattering drops of water and the air is stifling to breathe. But of real rain there is little. On that next morning, therefore, Miss Rachel saw with surprise that the wind was driving rain against her bedroom windows, fine small drops with a pebbly hardness.

The vagaries of California's weather were old stuff to Miss Rachel. She dressed warmly, went down for breakfast, and then, comfortably fed, she called Sheriff Butterworth on the telephone.

"I should like to talk with you," she told him. "As soon as possible."

He didn't shout with joy. "Something in regard to the murders?"

"That's right. I believe you'll find it interesting. By the way, may I ask if you've picked up Jerry Krythe?"

"No," said Butterworth. "We haven't tried very hard."

"I think you'd better put effort in the search. He's in dreadful danger. I'll explain when I see you."

"Dreadful danger," muttered Butterworth as if he were writing it down and didn't care much. "All right. I'll try to come out there sometime during the morning."

"Not—not right away?"

"Not right away," he said firmly.

Miss Jennifer being now at breakfast, Miss Rachel joined her for a second cup of coffee. Miriam's breakfast room was a round glass-enclosed porch, supposed to let in lots of sun and show a view of the lower valleys. This morning, with rain spattering the glass and thick clouds forming a gray pall overhead, the effect was not cheerful.

The maid who served them was big-eared and alert. Miss Rachel sent her for more toast before she spoke to Jennifer about Butterworth.

"And so he isn't coming right away," she concluded. "He thinks I'm trying to make him jump through hoops."

"He probably doesn't like nosy women either," said Jennifer.

"I wonder if he found that match folder I left under the doll?"

"I wouldn't know."

The maid returned. Miss Rachel asked her if Mr. Braudryck had been out yet. The maid said yes, that Mr. Braudryck was in Miriam's office that moment, going over papers there. He'd had coffee and toast sent in to him while he worked.

"Is his car parked out beside the garages?"

"I think he left it under the shelter there at the side entry," said the maid.

Miss Rachel sat silent for a long moment.

"Are you thinking?" asked Jennifer waspishly, "or has something fallen on your head? You have a quietly idiotic look."

"We might as well start the spadework," Miss Rachel said finally. "Jennifer, I'll need you." She turned to the maid with the big ears. "Ask Mr. Braudryck to meet us out beside his car. And call Checkers too."

"I hope you know what you're doing," said Jennifer. "Not like the time you put cleaning fluid in the glass Mrs. Farnsworth used for her false teeth at night."

"I knew Mrs. Farnsworth's teeth needed something. Only experiment showed that it wasn't cleaning fluid. Perhaps this experiment with Mr. Braudryck will leave as bad a taste. . . . Anyway, we'll see."

Under the porte-cochere Mr. Braudryck's car was long and gray and wetly shining. Miss Rachel tried the door handle, found that the car was locked.

Miss Jennifer coughed meaningly. Mr. Braudryck was coming out through the door. He didn't look happy and he did look as if he had a hangover. "You wanted me?"

"I'm investigating something in your car," said Miss Rachel brazenly. "Would you open it for me?"

He made no move to get his keys. "I've a damned good idea what you want. Butterworth routed me out last night about a match folder in the barn. The last two match folders I had were in my glove compartment. If you think I'm going to open up just for further framing you're mistaken."

Checkers came shuffling up the driveway. The maid with the big ears was listening solemnly from inside the hall.

Miss Rachel studied Mr. Braudryck's flushed, stubborn face. His slightly pouched eyes were venomous. "As a matter of fact I wasn't at all trying to frame you. You know that my sister and I found the doll in the barn at about midnight last night. I didn't see any match folder on the floor. This one, though"—she whipped out the folder which she had kept in her pocket—"this one was caught as if accidentally in a rip in the doll's dress. It was such an obvious, silly plant that I removed it. Now I return it to you." She put it into his hand.

Miss Jennifer made sputtering sounds over the outrageous lie, sounds which Mr. Braudryck no doubt took as an indication of sympathy for him.

"Well, you tampered with Butterworth's precious evidence," he grunted, "but you were right. It was a plant. I didn't have anything to do with that doll." His glance, much mollified, switched to his car. "What was it you wanted inside?"

"I've heard from another person that you carry some make-up kits in your glove compartment."

"From Mrs. Krythe?"

"She used to sell them in her store, didn't she?" asked Miss Rachel innocently. "Well, there are clues in them. Or, rather, out of them."

Mr. Braudryck took his keys from his coat pocket and moved toward the car. The maid came eagerly out upon the steps. Checkers, wearing an old slicker and a battered waterproof hat, stood quietly out in the rain. Miss Rachel turned to him suddenly.

"Checkers, we've lost our cat. Do bring her in if you find her. She's gray. Gray all over, except for little white feet."

His eyes, sightless or otherwise, seemed fixed intently on her own. He nodded his head slowly. "Was that all, ma'am?"

"Gray?" cried Miss Jennifer. "But——"

Miss Rachel gave her a look that caused her to snap her mouth shut angrily.

Mr. Braudryck had opened the car and brought out the three make-up kits. Miss Rachel took one from his hands, unsnapped the green imitation leather case to display the fitted interior. She lifted the lid of the powder box. It was full, so full that powder spilled out upon her hand. The rouge was new, unused. She unscrewed the cap of the green plastic cylinder holding lipstick.

"Empty," she said, showing it to Mr. Braudryck.

" 'S funny," said Mr. Braudryck. "That's the blond case, isn't it? I don't even know any blondes."

"Let's try redhead," said Miss Rachel. Again the powder box was full, the rouge new, the lipstick empty.

Mr. Braudryck was frowning. "Looks as if there's been a lot of wear and tear in one direction. Only I'm not quite that active. After all, being a lawyer takes a *little* time."

Miss Jennifer fixed him with her best Ladies' Aid stare.

Mr. Braudryck himself opened the last case, examined its contents with what seemed to be genuine puzzlement. "I don't get it. You said there were clues here."

"Did you see the doll that was used in the attempt to terrify Miriam? I mean, last night when Butterworth routed you out, did he show it to you?"

"He had it with him. It was ghastly all right."

"Had he identified the bright red stain that seemed to have leaked from its broken head?"

"No, I guess not. He didn't say. Wait. You mean these lipsticks——"

Sharon had come out upon the steps and sent the maid on some errand. She looked tired, tense, and there were touches of blue color under the skin about her eyes. She stood listening to what Braudryck said.

"I think your three lipsticks were melted down and used to make the gory-looking mess on the doll's hair and face," said Miss Rachel. She was poking, searching the case in her hands as if for something more. The little stitched pockets in the lining which she had noted before seemed suddenly to attract her attention. "These," she said abruptly, opening one of the little pockets. "What originally were in these compartments?"

"Why . . . I guess I don't remember. I bought them from Mrs. Krythe one day, just sort of helping out, see? I knew she was hard up. Maybe a comb? No, guess it isn't big enough."

Checkers was rubbing his seamed hands together under the cuffs of the old raincoat. His almost sightless eyes roved from one person to another. Perhaps figures were large enough, distinct enough, for him to see. He had not seemed to look directly at the little make-up kits.

Sharon turned to glance behind her. Joe Dewel had come out from the house. He was wearing an old overcoat, and a disreputable felt hat covered with raindrops, hung from one hand. "Hello," he said. "Here I come begging breakfast and run into a conference. What are we this morning: a bunch of Sherlocks? Watson, the needle, and all that."

Braudryck didn't look up at him. He went on staring at the little case in Miss Rachel's hands. The rain, blown by the wind, made fitful excursions into the space under the porte-cochere. It sizzled on Checkers's raincoat, but he made no move to come into the shelter with the others.

"I know now," said Braudryck. "There were little mirrors in those pockets. I remember using one once to get a speck of dirt out of my eye." He searched the pocket in the case he held. "And the mirrors are gone. All three of them."

There was silence when he had stopped speaking. Into that silence came the light sound of footsteps. At the end of the graveled drive, where it curved toward the garages, appeared the figure of Jerry Krythe. He was wrapped in a yellow oilskin. His young face was grim and anxious.

Checkers had turned with the others. Now he cried hoarsely: "Who is it? Who's coming? Jerry?"

"Yeah," said Jerry, still some distance away. Rain had frosted his sandy eyebrows and his lashes. His freckles stood out in a white face. "I'm looking for my mother."

"Go back!" Checkers cried. "Go away! I'll meet you somewhere. I'll tell you about your mother."

Jerry had paused, puzzled. Sharon and Joe Dewel had come down from the steps in order to see the length of the drive. Mr. Braudryck was looking at Checkers with suspicion.

"I'll meet you in an hour at the place we met last night," said Checkers desperately.

"No, Jerry," said Miss Rachel gently. "Don't go. You needn't be afraid here."

Jerry advanced an uncertain step. Checkers seemed to shudder inside the old raincoat. He turned his head from side to side as if seeking escape.

"Why shouldn't I stay here?" demanded Jerry. "And if you know where my mother is, why don't you tell me?" He was almost at Checkers's side now. "Tell me."

"I'm—I'm right here, Jerry," said an apologetic voice. The group turned. Mrs. Krythe had come toward the front of the house. She had on a cheap, transparent hooded raincoat, and under it showed the shabby gray coat, the pulled-down hat, and the fringe of fuzzy hair. "Butterworth came looking for you. He said you might be in danger."

"In danger?" Jerry echoed. His eyes searched the faces of the others. "Who from? Somebody here?"

A sudden tension and stillness gripped them all. Miss Rachel moved softly, putting herself between Jerry and the group. The rain, blowing harder, frosted her hair with a silver mist. Jerry's expression had become a little afraid.

"You have a very important part of the evidence relating to the murders," she said quietly. "We need that, Jerry—we need *the three mirrors* you picked up in the grove."

He looked warily about. "Who told you I had them?"

"We just knew," she said calmly. "And we have to have them in order to know the truth."

He shook his head. "I've been thinking about those mirrors and what they might mean. Maybe they'll get a friend of mine in trouble."

Checkers had shrunk back into the hedge that separated the house from the driveway. On his face had appeared a greenish color and one eyelid twitched in a series of nervous spasms.

Sharon said incredulously, "Mirrors? Where?"

"Jerry found three mirrors on the cut off path, lying on the ground about twenty feet apart."

"Like somebody'd dropped them," Jerry supplied mechanically.

"No, Jerry. Not like somebody had dropped them. Just put there, reflecting light. Three bright spots marking the path that helped the murderer get away in a hurry."

"I don't get it," said Mr. Braudryck. "*Three mirrors . . .*"

"Someone found good use for your make-up kits," said Miss Rachel. "The lipstick went to fix the doll. Then when mirrors were needed the murderer remembered." She turned, looked at everyone except Checkers, crouched against the hedge. "Do any of you remember the old story about the boy who went into the maze and found his way out again by means of a string he had brought with him on his way in?"

"Old yarn from mythology, wasn't it?" said Joe Dewel. "Was that a pun?"

"You mean," said Braudryck, "that the murderer had to leave and find that path quickly and wasn't familiar enough with it . . . No. Wait a minute. I know what you're driving at. *The three bright points.*" He was staring incredulously at Checkers. "The lath house. The tin lids. *Checkers!*"

The bent figure had bounded forth from the hedge and was pounding down the graveled driveway. Mrs. Krythe let out a sobbing cry. Jerry stood rooted, unmoving.

"I'll stop him!" said Joe Dewel, and bent to reach for a rock in the border under the hedge.

But no one had to stop Checkers. He had reached the driveway and struck off across the open space that led to the corral. He found the corral fence and began to feel his way along it. Then, as if no longer able to control himself, he tried to climb. He reached the top bar, put a leg over it, stopped there tottering.

Joe Dewel drew back his arm to throw and Miss Rachel seized his elbow. "Wait," she cried.

Through the gray mist made by the blowing rain they saw Checkers flail his arms and then go over. Apparently he struck his head. After he had fallen there was no movement from the heap inside the raincoat.

# CHAPTER TWENTY

MR. BRAUDRYCK and Jerry carried the limp figure of Checkers into the house. Sharon led the way to the living room, helped take off Checkers's coat and straighten him on one of Miriam's big yellow velvet couches. He lay there looking small and old and shriveled. Sharon touched his cold cheek softly. "Poor Checkers," she whispered. Blood had clotted in a cut above his temple. He didn't move at Sharon's touch, didn't open his eyes.

"Do you think he's shamming?" asked Joe Dewel.

"Perhaps not," said Miss Rachel gently.

Mrs. Krythe came in from the hall. She took in the bigness of the room, the sea of pale lilac carpeting, the two grand pianos in front of the high window, with a single scornful glance. Then she went to sit beside Checkers in a yellow chair.

"I'll go call Butterworth," said Mr. Braudryck, leaving the room.

Sharon had turned to Miss Rachel. "Is it true? Did Checkers kill Miriam and Bart?"

"Think it out for yourself," said Miss Rachel. "Think of the ways the crimes were alike, and the manner in which each point fitted Checkers. Take weapons for example. In each case the weapon was something close at hand, something that didn't have to be brought from the village, something even an almost blind man could use."

"I wish Butterworth were here," said Joe Dewel. "He ought to have figured that all out for himself."

"At first the weapon used to murder Mr. Dewel seemed unwieldy, even grotesque; and I kept wondering why it should have been used when knives are cheap and available. Then it occurred to me that if the murderer had to *make a weapon*—had to use just what was at hand—the long needle and the doll's arm were about the best he could do."

"I agree with Mr. Dewel. You should wait for Sheriff Butterworth before going into this," said Miss Jennifer.

Mr. Braudryck returned at this moment. "The sheriff must be on his way here. The deputy in his office said he left some fifteen minutes ago."

"Naturally," said Joe Dewel, staring at Checkers's still figure, "the old man couldn't go shopping for knives in the shape he was in. He'd have to do with what he had."

Miss Rachel nodded agreement. "Also . . . think of the manner of Miriam's murder. *Murder in the dark.* Who but a man nearly blind, used to an almost complete darkness all of the time, would have moved surely and swiftly enough to commit the crime?" She turned suddenly to Mrs. Krythe. "You acted strangely in the theater when I mentioned *the little light.* I was speaking of light being thrown on the case. I think the remark caused you to recall another light, perhaps the one Checkers lit in the barn two nights ago."

Mrs. Krythe stared at her voicelessly.

"When he lit the match you may have seen something—perhaps Miriam's eyes at the crack of the divided door that leads to the lath house and was folded back against the wall."

Mrs. Krythe's thin throat moved in a convulsive swallowing motion. She licked her dry lips. Her hands plucked at the fastenings of the cheap transparent raincoat. "I—I might as well admit it. Yes, I did guess that Mrs. Hamilton was listening. I saw eyes shining in the strip between the two halves of the door. The corner of a black fur cuff was sticking out at one side."

Mr. Braudryck had been listening intently. "Since it all adds up now, I'll tell what Miriam talked about on the terrace that night. She was still going after Rick. In addition she was jubilant over some other discovery. I guessed she'd caught someone out in something he shouldn't have done. That person must have been Checkers."

"Yeah." Mr. Joe Dewel's eyes were full of puzzled anger. "And come to think of it—what kind of person would Bart have let come close enough to stab him in the brain? Remember, he was writing something to expose the murderer. He'd want to frighten that person if his object had been blackmail. Well . . . he'd let a half-blind man come and stick his head over his shoulder, wouldn't he? Unsuspecting. It's as clear as daylight."

Sheriff Butterworth strode into the room. He wore his business suit and his air of being a prosperous store owner out to make a sharp bargain. A gray waterproof coat hung over his arm.

Mr. Braudryck indicated Checkers, stretched out on the couch. "Here's your man, Butterworth. Strange as it is, all the evidence points to him. Even motive—with Jerry Krythe out of the way, he'd have a better chance of marrying Mrs. Krythe and sharing Dave's estate. We've been talking things over. You'll get a conviction without any trouble."

As though the words were a cue, Checkers sat up groggily and touched his forehead with a trembling hand. "Fell, didn't I?" he croaked. "Where is this? Am I inside somewhere?"

"You're in the house," said Sharon gently. She turned impulsively to Butterworth. "Shouldn't he be looked over by a doctor? He's hurt himself."

"Trying to get away," sneered Joe Dewel. "Let the doctor look him over in jail."

"He isn't going to jail," said Miss Rachel quietly. "Because, you see, in spite of all the carefully manufactured evidence—*Checkers didn't commit any murders!*"

There was tight-strung, breathless silence for a moment. The sheriff's eyes were searching the group like a ferret's. Mr. Braudryck touched his tie nervously. Mrs. Krythe sat straight and very still. Then Miss Jennifer burst forth with: "Well, Rachel . . . now we see you, now we don't. Are you a rabbit in a hat?"

"I've an inquiring mind," Miss Rachel admitted modestly, "and so after I'd sorted and weighed all the evidence against Checkers I thought there were one or two little items that the theory about Checkers didn't cover. So I went on mentally inquiring about them."

"Such as?" asked Butterworth.

"Well . . . the whole structure of Checkers's guilt depended on his near blindness. The mirrors which Jerry found marking the trail . . ." She digressed briefly to outline the sketch to the sheriff. "And the whole manner of Bart Dewel's murder. The kind of weapons."

"Checkers *is* almost blind," said Sharon.

Miss Rachel nodded. "Yes. Even blinder than the rest of us had guessed. He knew by sound, for example, that I had a cat which followed me. He couldn't see well enough to know its color, though it must have been less than five feet from him. You note he didn't correct me a few minutes ago in the driveway, when I called the cat *gray* to test him."

"Don't forget the four white feet," snapped Miss Jennifer. "When you're lying, Rachel, you always add embellishments."

"He might have sensed a trap," said Joe Dewel.

"Yes, he might. But note his behavior at the fence, when he was trying desperately to get away. He couldn't see well enough to climb safely, to reach the ground without falling."

"I shouldn't have run," moaned Checkers. "Couldn't see. Felt something closing in. . . ."

"You felt the lies of the murderer closing in," said Miss Rachel. "And you were blind and afraid. But your blindness is going to save you—that plus a couple of slips made by the murderer."

Mrs. Krythe seemed to wish to rise from the yellow chair. She put out a clenched, nervous hand, gathered her feet under her. Her eyes flitted from person to person as if weighing, questioning.

"Take, for instance, the use of the long needle and the doll's hand in the murder of Bart Dewel. This seemed like the impromptu weapon making of someone restricted in scope of movement, like Checkers. Only . . . Sharon took the needle to the Hamilton house. *The murderer took only the doll's hand.*"

The queer, singing silence returned. Mr. Braudryck went on loosening his tie. Mrs. Krythe's pose assumed a crouched appearance.

"You see, then, that the murderer had to know that Sharon had carried the needle with her. It is true that on the way she paused to speak with Checkers, *but at a distance of at least fifteen feet.*"

"Checkers couldn't have seen a needle at that distance," said Butterworth. "I guess someone with normal vision though . . ."

"Remember that on the terrace, at approximately the same distance, we saw the needle that Mrs. Krythe had dropped."

Butterworth's air of being a shrewd businessman left him suddenly. He hunched his shoulders, edged forward toward the others. "Who else, then, saw Sharon Hamilton going to the studio?"

"Rick can tell you that," said Miss Rachel.

She saw Butterworth's mind struggling with the details of Rick's story. She went on swiftly. "The murderer made other errors. He described a visit to Mrs. Hamilton's bedroom which was supposed to have taken place some years ago, and in this story he mentioned a handmade lace spread which is new . . . and which wouldn't have been on the bed while Miriam was in it, anyway, but would have been replaced by her down quilt. Ask Miriam's maid for the details. She'll point out to you the errors made by the person who brought Miriam in from the barn and put her into bed."

Mr. Joe Dewel was breathing hoarsely. One hand had strayed to the pocket of his overcoat, was fingering something there.

"One final, clinching detail. . . . Have you mentioned to anyone except me the fact that Bart Dewel was writing a letter at the time of his death?"

"No one," said Butterworth. He swung slowly on Joe Dewel. "What's wrong with you, man?"

Mr. Braudryck was pointing with a shaking finger. "*He* told us about the letter writing!"

Joe Dewel's clenched hand came out of his pocket holding a businesslike little automatic. Like himself, the gun was a trifle seedy and rusty, and like him, also, it was full of cold-blooded unregretful murder.

"Just relax, folks. I'm going to leave you now. It won't be healthy for the first few who try to follow. Don't try to telephone. I'm going to take care of that on my way out."

Butterworth didn't move but his steel-colored eyes studied Joe Dewel contemptuously. "You're crazy, man. You'll never make a getaway on foot."

"Who said anything about on foot? Braudryck, toss your keys over."

"No," said Mr. Braudryck weakly. "No, I won't have my car shot up in a chase. I—oh well. Here."

The jutting muzzle of the gun had convinced him. He threw Joe Dewel his keys.

Checkers was trying to get to his feet. "I can't see. Is everybody still here? Mr. Dewel, you leaving?"

"Right now," said Joe Dewel, backing toward the door. "Sorry about the frame-up, Checkers. It didn't start out that way. If I could have gained time by that trick of bringing Miriam in, kept them from finding out how she died . . . There was evidence I'd been in the tractor."

"One last moment. Tell us why you killed Miriam!" cried Miss Rachel.

"I ought to let you have this instead," Dewel ground out, pointing the black muzzle her way. "But if it makes you happier . . . some of those confidential missions didn't turn out so well from Mrs. Hamilton's point of view. They put some much-needed dough in my pockets. As for all that sob story about my kid being in Stanford . . ." He laughed shortly, bitterly. "He's out, he's got a good job a long way from here, where nothing of all this can reach him. Anyway, the kid wasn't the real reason I took on Miriam's footwork. I thought I'd have a chance to turn things my way, and I did. When I overheard her and Braudryck on the terrace that night I knew she meant me. . . . I knew the funny business with the doll and the fuchsias wasn't going to keep her in line. I slipped away and waited. Catching her behind that door in the dark was pure luck. You see, she waited a little too long after Checkers and Mrs. Krythe left. And you weren't the only one outside in the dark, looking in, when that match was lit."

He had reached the doorway.

"Mr. Dewel," Checkers stammered, "I can't believe you'd murder your own brother."

"My brother," said Joe Dewel with a kind of slow ferocity, "knew that Ray Hamilton had left that doll with me. He also knew that I'd gotten oil on a pair of trousers, climbing into that tractor seat in the dark. The blackmailing skunk thought I ought to kick through with a little of what I'd gotten out of my undercover work for Miriam."

He was reaching behind him for the doorknob.

"Mr. Dewel," said Miss Rachel sharply, "my cat is just behind your heel. Please don't step on her."

The sharp, commanding tone cut across his mood of absorbed watchfulness. Involuntarily he looked behind him at the floor. It was an old, utterly simple trick. Only the downright reasonableness of Miss Rachel's cat having come into the room made him turn.

Behind him the lilac turf was empty. He swung back viciously—to meet Butterworth's big shining Colt.

For an instant that seemed forever a hint of indecision flickered in his eyes. Then he made a prodding movement with his right hand and the gun sang. But Butterworth's big Colt roared at almost the same moment.

Joe Dewel backed against the door. A glassy mockery settled in his face. "Don't cry over me, folks. Just toast my memory in the best champagne. . . ." His bubbling, chirruping tone ended in a spasm of coughing. His legs buckled and he fell sidewise.

Something hard and dark and shining spilled from his pocket in a heap.

"The wisteria seeds," cried Miss Jennifer, covering her eyes.

Miss Rachel gathered them from the floor when the body of Joe Dewel had been carried away. "I've always wanted a wisteria vine," she said softly to Jennifer.

"You can't want *those!*"

"Why not? After all they didn't choose Mr. Dewel."

"They'll remind you of murder!"

"Not half so much as Aunt Lily's rhinestone garters."

"Rachel!"

"Please, Jennifer. Why were you poking about in those boilers?"

Miss Jennifer looked about to make sure that they were alone. "I overheard Mr. Braudryck make the queerest remark. I was in the little sitting room, and Mr. Braudryck and the sheriff were on the terrace . . . and Mr. Braudryck said he believed he could solve the case if he had the help of a couple of boilermakers."

*"Boilermakers?"*

"That's right. So naturally I went looking for boilers. You aren't the only one who can play at being a detective, Rachel. Only, of course, I didn't find anything."

Miss Rachel was beset with indecision. Should she tell Jennifer what the alcoholically inclined Mr. Braudryck meant by a couple of boilermakers? Or should she just discreetly keep still? Explaining the mystery to Jennifer might lead to complications—perhaps even the revelation of the episode in the bar, the hefty drink Mr. Braudryck had prepared for her, the fact that she had woozily taken Jennifer herself for the—what was the expression now?—the *D.T.s.*

Miss Jennifer would certainly not like being taken for the *D.T.s.*

Miss Rachel just discreetly kept still.

THE END

## DISCUSSION QUESTIONS

- Did any aspects of the plot date the story? If so, which?
- Would the story be different if it were set in the present day? If so, how?
- Did the social context of the time play a role in the narrative? If so, how?
- If you were one of the main characters, would you have acted differently at any point in the story?
- Did you identify with any of the characters? If so, which?
- What skills or qualities make Rachel Murdock such an effective sleuth?
- Did this book remind you of any present day authors? If so, which?

## OTTO PENZLER PRESENTS
# AMERICAN MYSTERY CLASSICS

*All titles are available in hardcover and in trade paperback.*

Order from your favorite bookstore or from
The Mysterious Bookshop, 58 Warren Street, New York, N.Y. 10007
(www.mysteriousbookshop.com).

**Charlotte Armstrong, *The Chocolate Cobweb.*** When Amanda Garth was born, a mix-up caused the hospital to briefly hand her over to the prestigious Garrison family instead of to her birth parents. The error was quickly fixed, Amanda was never told, and the secret was forgotten for twenty-three years . . . until her aunt revealed it in casual conversation. But what if the initial switch never actually occurred? **Introduction by A. J. Finn.**

**Charlotte Armstrong, *The Unsuspected.*** First published in 1946, this suspenseful novel opens with a young woman who has ostensibly hanged herself, leaving a suicide note. Her friend doesn't believe it and begins an investigation that puts her own life in jeopardy. It was filmed in 1947 by Warner Brothers, starring Claude Rains and Joan Caulfield. **Introduction by Otto Penzler.**

**Anthony Boucher, *The Case of the Baker Street Irregulars.*** When a studio announces a new hard-boiled Sherlock Holmes film, the Baker Street Irregulars begin a campaign to discredit it. Attempting to mollify them, the producers invite members to the set, where threats are received, each referring to one of the original Holmes tales, followed by murder. Fortunately, the amateur sleuths use Holmesian lessons to solve the crime. **Introduction by Otto Penzler.**

**Anthony Boucher, *Rocket to the Morgue.*** Hilary Foulkes has made so many enemies that it is difficult to speculate who was responsible for stabbing him nearly to death in a room with only one door through which no one was seen entering or leaving. This classic locked room mystery is populated by such thinly disguised science fiction legends as Robert Heinlein, L. Ron Hubbard, and John W. Campbell. **Introduction by F. Paul Wilson.**

**Fredric Brown, *The Fabulous Clipjoint.*** Brown's outstanding mystery won an Edgar as the best first novel of the year (1947). When Wallace Hunter is found dead in an alley after a long night of drinking, the police don't really care. But his teenage son Ed and his uncle Am, the carnival worker, are convinced that some things don't add up and the crime isn't what it seems to be. **Introduction by Lawrence Block.**

**John Dickson Carr, *The Burning Court.*** When Edward Stevens learns of the mysterious events that befell his neighbor's rich uncle, he shrugs off their seemingly supernatural circumstances. But as suspicions of strange murder begin to creep in, it becomes harder for Stevens to ignore their eerie potential. Unsettling echoes of the past into the present push things even further past Stevens' understanding of reality. **Introduction by Dan Napolitano.**

**John Dickson Carr, *The Crooked Hinge.*** Selected by a group of mystery experts as one of the 15 best impossible crime novels ever written, this is one of Gideon Fell's greatest challenges. Estranged from his family for 25 years, Sir John Farnleigh returns to England from America to claim his inheritance but another person turns up claiming that he can prove he is the real Sir John. Inevitably, one of them is murdered. **Introduction by Charles Todd.**

**John Dickson Carr, *The Eight of Swords.*** When Gideon Fell arrives at a crime scene, it appears to be straightforward enough. A man has been shot to death in an unlocked room and the likely perpetrator was a recent visitor. But Fell discovers inconsistencies and his investigations are complicated by an apparent poltergeist, some American gangsters, and two meddling amateur sleuths. **Introduction by Otto Penzler.**

**John Dickson Carr, *The Mad Hatter Mystery.*** A prankster has been stealing top hats all around London. Gideon Fell suspects that the same person may be responsible for the theft of a manuscript of a long-lost story by Edgar Allan Poe. The hats reappear in unexpected but conspicuous places. But when one is found on the head of a corpse by the Tower of London, it is evident that the thefts are more than pranks. **Introduction by Otto Penzler.**

**John Dickson Carr, *The Plague Court Murders.*** When murder occurs in a locked hut on Plague Court, an estate haunted by the ghost of a hangman's assistant who died a victim of the black death, Sir Henry Merrivale seeks a logical solution to a ghostly crime. A spiritual medium employed to rid the house of his spirit is found stabbed to death in a locked stone hut on the grounds, surrounded by an untouched circle of mud. **Introduction by Michael Dirda.**

**John Dickson Carr, *The Problem of the Wire Cage.*** Death and tennis collide in one of this impossible crime master's most memorable cases. After a storm, a man lies strangled on a clay tennis court with no footprints on the damp ground other than his own. This puzzle requires ace amateur sleuth Dr. Gideon Fell to serve up a dazzling stroke of genius to outplay the culprit. **Introduction by Rian Johnson.**

**John Dickson Carr, *The Red Widow Murders.*** In a "haunted" mansion, the room known as the Red Widow's Chamber proves lethal to all who spend the night. Eight people investigate and the one who draws the ace of spades must sleep in the cursed bedroom. The room is locked from the inside and watched all night by the others. When the door is unlocked, the victim has been poisoned. Enter Sir Henry Merrivale to solve the crime. **Introduction by Tom Mead.**

**John Dickson Carr, *The Three Coffins*.** Called *The Hollow Man* in the UK, this tale was voted the best locked room mystery of all time by a 1981 survey of mystery experts. Dr. Gideon Fell sets out to solve two impossible murders: A professor is found dead in his study just moments after his housekeeper watched him greet a mysterious visitor and an illusionist is shot in the snow with no footprints nearby but his own. **Introduction by Otto Penzler.**

**Frances Crane, *The Turquoise Shop.*** In an arty little New Mexico town, Mona Brandon has arrived from the East and becomes the subject of gossip about her money, her influence, and the corpse in the nearby desert who may be her husband. Pat Holly, who runs the local gift shop, is as interested as anyone in the goings on—but even more in Pat Abbott, the detective investigating the possible murder. **Introduction by Anne Hillerman.**

**Todd Downing, *Vultures in the Sky.*** There is no end to the series of terrifying events that befall a luxury train bound for Mexico. First, a man dies when the train passes through a dark tunnel. Then the train comes to an abrupt stop in the middle of the desert. More deaths occur when night falls and the passengers panic as they realize they are trapped with a murderer on the loose. **Introduction by James Sallis.**

**Mignon G. Eberhart, *Murder by an Aristocrat.*** Nurse Keate is called to help a man who has been "accidentally" shot in the shoulder. When he is murdered while convalescing, it is clear that there was no accident. Although a killer is loose in the mansion, the family seems more concerned that news of the murder will leave their circle. *The New Yorker* wrote that "Eberhart can weave an almost flawless mystery." **Introduction by Nancy Pickard.**

**Mignon G. Eberhart, *While The Patient Slept*.** From the moment nurse Sarah Keate arrives at the gloomy mansion of Adolph Federie, she senses trouble afoot. But Mr. Federie has just suffered a stroke and needs a live-in aid and Sarah is not one to shirk her duties. When a murder occurs in the same room as her patient, Sarah starts investigating. But how will she sleep at night knowing she's sharing a house with a killer? **Introduction by Lisa Unger.**

**Stanley Ellin, *Dreadful Summit*.** Sixteen-year-old George LaMain is hard-bitten reporter Al Judge's biggest fan—until the night his own father becomes the target of the journalist's attacks. Reeling from a moment that upends his whole worldview, George takes his father's gun and sets out into the night on a quest for revenge. But before he can achieve justice, the young man discovers an unsettling truth about the family he thought he knew. **Introduction by Andrew Klavan.**

**Erle Stanley Gardner, *The Bigger They Come*** .Gardner's first novel using the pseudonym A.A. Fair begins a series featuring the large and loud Bertha Cool and her employee, the small and meek Donald Lam. Given the job of delivering divorce papers to an evident crook, Lam can't find him—but neither can the police. The *Los Angeles Times* called this book "breathlessly dramatic . . . an original." **Introduction by Otto Penzler.**

**Erle Stanley Gardner, *The Case of the Baited Hook.*** Perry Mason gets a phone call in the middle of the night and his potential client says it's urgent, that he has two one-thousand-dollar bills that he will give him as a retainer, with an additional ten-thousand whenever he is called on to represent him. When

Mason takes the case, it is not for the caller but for a beautiful woman whose identity is hidden behind a mask. **Introduction by Otto Penzler.**

**Erle Stanley Gardner, *The Case of the Borrowed Brunette.*** A mysterious man named Mr. Hines has advertised a job for a woman who has to fulfill very specific physical requirements. Eva Martell, pretty but struggling in her career as a model, takes the job but her aunt smells a rat and hires Perry Mason to investigate. Her fears are realized when Hines turns up in the apartment with a bullet hole in his head. **Introduction by Otto Penzler.**

**Erle Stanley Gardner, *The Case of the Careless Kitten.*** Helen Kendal receives a mysterious phone call from her vanished uncle Franklin, long presumed dead, who urges her to contact Perry Mason. Soon, she finds herself the main suspect in the murder of an unfamiliar man. Her kitten has just survived a poisoning attempt—as has her aunt Matilda. What is the connection between Franklin's return and the attempted murders? **Introduction by Otto Penzler.**

**Erle Stanley Gardner, *The Case of the Rolling Bones.*** One of Gardner's most successful Perry Mason novels opens with a clear case of blackmail, though the person being blackmailed claims he isn't. It is not long before the police are searching for someone wanted for killing the same man in two different states—thirty-three years apart. The confounding puzzle of what happened to the dead man's toes is a challenge. **Introduction by Otto Penzler.**

**Erle Stanley Gardner, *The Case of the Shoplifter's Shoe.*** Most cases for Perry Mason involve murder but here he is hired because a young woman fears her aunt is a kleptomaniac. Sarah may not have been precisely the best guardian for a collection of valuable diamonds and, sure enough, they go missing. When the jeweler is found shot dead, Sarah is spotted leaving the murder scene with a bundle of gems stuffed in her purse. **Introduction by Otto Penzler.**

**Erle Stanley Gardner, *The D.A. Calls It Murder*.** In a small town north of Los Angeles, Doug Selby claims narrow victory in a hotly contested race for District Attorney. Then his troubles begin: The local paper immediately launches an effort to get Selby recalled. Then a murdered man is found in Selby's campaign headquarters. A fast-paced and twisty investigation ensues, involving a famous actress, a stolen identity, and plenty of red herrings as Selby endeavors to determine whodunit. **Introduction by Otto Penzler.**

**Frances Noyes Hart, *The Bellamy Trial.*** Inspired by the real-life Hall-Mills case, the most sensational trial of its day, this is the story of Stephen Bellamy and Susan Ives, accused of murdering Bellamy's wife Madeleine. Eight days of dynamic testimony, some true, some not, make headlines for an enthralled public. Rex Stout called this historic courtroom thriller one of the ten best mysteries of all time. **Introduction by Hank Phillippi Ryan.**

**H.F. Heard, *A Taste for Honey.*** The elderly Mr. Mycroft quietly keeps bees in Sussex, where he is approached by the reclusive and somewhat misanthropic Mr. Silchester, whose honey supplier was found dead, stung to death by her bees. Mycroft, who shares many traits with Sherlock Holmes, sets out to find the vicious killer. Rex Stout described it as "sinister . . . a tale well and truly told." **Introduction by Otto Penzler.**

**Dolores Hitchens, *The Alarm of the Black Cat.*** Detective fiction aficionado Rachel Murdock has a peculiar meeting with a little girl and a dead toad, sparking her curiosity about a love triangle that has sparked anger. When the girl's great grandmother is found dead, Rachel and her cat Samantha work with a friend in the Los Angeles Police Department to get to the bottom of things. **Introduction by David Handler.**

**Dolores Hitchens, *The Cat Saw Murder.*** Miss Rachel Murdock, the highly intelligent 70-year-old amateur sleuth, is not entirely heartbroken when her slovenly, unattractive, bridge-cheating niece is murdered. Miss Rachel is happy to help the socially maladroit and somewhat bumbling Detective Lieutenant Stephen Mayhew, retaining her composure when a second brutal murder occurs. **Introduction by Joyce Carol Oates.**

**Dolores Hitchens, *Cat's Claw.*** Miss Rachel Murdock, the elderly amateur sleuth, can't help but be intrigued by a murder method so shocking and by the baffling developments that follow. The ensuing investigation takes Miss Rachel and her cat Samantha to a small mountain town and into a property conflict with deadly potential. Will she be able to determine whodunit before the killer strikes again? **Introduction by Katherine Hall Page.**

**Dolores Hitchens, *The Cat Wears a Noose*.** Walking home, Jennifer Murdock sees a drunk man shot dead on his doorstep. A young girl from that house on Chestnut Street then seeks the help of Jennifer's sister Rachel, a vigorous senior sleuth, after a series of nasty pranks culminate in her pet bird's death. Neither her prim and proper sister nor Det. Lt. Mayhew can stop Rachel from finding out what is going on. **Introduction by Rhys Bowen.**

**Dorothy B. Hughes, *Dread Journey*.** A big-shot Hollywood producer has worked on his magnum opus for years, hiring and firing one beautiful starlet after another. But Kitten Agnew's contract won't allow her to be fired, so she fears she might be terminated more permanently. Together with the producer on a train journey from Hollywood to Chicago, Kitten becomes more terrified with each passing mile. **Introduction by Sarah Weinman.**

**Dorothy B. Hughes, *The Fallen Sparrow*.** When Kit McKittrick learns that his friend Louie has taken a long dive out of a high window, he refuses to believe it was a suicide and sets out on a quest for vengeance that leads him to wrestle with past demons from his time spent in a Spanish prison. It was adapted into a now-classic film noir starring John Garfield and Maureen O'Hara. **Introduction by Otto Penzler.**

**Dorothy B. Hughes, *Ride the Pink Horse*.** When Sailor met Willis Douglass, he was just a poor kid who Douglass groomed to work as a confidential secretary. As the senator became increasingly corrupt, he knew he could count on Sailor to clean up his messes. No longer a senator, Douglass flees Chicago for Santa Fe, leaving behind a murder rap and Sailor as the prime suspect. Seeking vengeance, Sailor follows. **Introduction by Sara Paretsky.**

**Dorothy B. Hughes, *The So Blue Marble*.** Set in the glamorous world of New York high society, this novel became a suspense classic as twins from Europe try to steal a rare and beautiful gem owned by an aristocrat whose sister is an even more menacing presence. *The New Yorker* called it "extraordinary . . . [Hughes'] brilliant descriptive powers make and unmake reality." **Introduction by Otto Penzler.**

**W. Bolingbroke Johnson, *The Widening Stain*.** After a cocktail party, the attractive Lucie Coindreau, a "black-eyed, black-haired Frenchwoman" visits the rare books wing of the library and apparently takes a headfirst fall from an upper gallery. Dismissed as a horrible accident, it seems dubious when Professor Hyett is strangled while reading a priceless 12th-century manuscript, which has gone missing. **Introduction by Nicholas A. Basbanes.**

**Baynard Kendrick, *Blind Man's Bluff*.** Blinded in World War II, Duncan Maclain forms a successful private detective agency, aided by his two dogs. Here, he is called on to solve the case of a blind man who plummets from the top of an eight-story building, apparently with no one present except his dead-drunk son. **Introduction by Otto Penzler.**

**Baynard Kendrick, *The Odor of Violets*.** Duncan Maclain, a blind former intelligence officer, is asked to investigate the murder of an actor in his Greenwich Village apartment. This would cause a stir at any time but, when the actor possesses secret government plans that then go missing, it's enough to interest the local police as well as the American government and Maclain, who suspects a German spy plot. **Introduction by Otto Penzler.**

**C. Daly King, *Obelists at Sea*.** On a cruise ship traveling from New York to Paris, the lights of the smoking room briefly go out, a gunshot crashes through the night, and a man is dead. Two detectives are on board but so are four psychiatrists who believe their professional knowledge can solve the case by understanding the psyche of the killer—each with a different theory. **Introduction by Martin Edwards.**

**C. Daly King, *Obelists en Route*.** The magnificent Transcontinental Express is making its first trip from New York to San Francisco. Among refined staterooms and elegant cars, the train's most lauded feature is a swimming pool—which is where the corpse of a prominent banker is discovered just one day into the journey. A select group of passengers, including the sharp-witted Dr. Pons, are tasked with uncovering what has occurred. **Introduction by Otto Penzler.**

**C. Daly King, *Obelists Fly High*.** A surgeon aboard a transcontinental flight is found murdered, having received a threat to his life just prior to boarding. Though the only suspects are confined to the plane, none say they saw anything. This is the conundrum facing NYPD Detective Michael Lord before he, too, is threatened. Fortunately, he is accompanied by his friend, Dr. Rees Pons, who aids him in this whodunit mystery. **Introduction by Otto Penzler.**

**Rufus King, *Murder by the Clock*.** Herbert Endicott is discovered dead in his walk-in closet. Lieutenant Valcour, New York's most astute investigator, orders an autopsy on site and the doctor discovers a faint heartbeat. With an injection of adrenaline, Endicott is awake. But just a few hours later, he's shot dead—this time for good. From this puzzling set-up, an atmospheric and tense mystery ensues, with Valcour turning up more questions than answers. **Introduction by Kelli Stanley.**

**Jonathan Latimer, *Headed for a Hearse*.** Featuring Bill Crane, the booze-soaked Chicago private detective, this humorous hard-boiled novel was filmed as *The Westland Case* in 1937 starring Preston Foster. Robert Westland has been framed for the grisly murder of his wife in a room with doors and windows locked from the inside. As the day of his execution nears, he relies on Crane to find the real murderer. **Introduction by Max Allan Collins.**

**Lange Lewis, *The Birthday Murder*.** Victoria is a successful novelist and screenwriter and her husband is a movie director, so their marriage seems almost too good to be true. Then, on her birthday, her happy new life comes crashing down when her husband is murdered using a method of poisoning that was described in one of her books. She quickly becomes the leading suspect. **Introduction by Randal S. Brandt.**

**Frances and Richard Lockridge, *Death on the Aisle*.** In one of the most beloved books to feature Mr. and Mrs. North, the body of a wealthy backer of a play is found dead in a seat of the 45th Street Theater. Pam is thrilled to engage in her favorite pastime—playing amateur sleuth—much to the annoyance of Jerry, her publisher husband. The Norths inspired a stage play, a film, and long-running radio and TV series. **Introduction by Otto Penzler.**

**John P. Marquand, *Your Turn, Mr. Moto*.** The first novel about Mr. Moto, originally titled *No Hero*, is the story of a World War I hero pilot who finds himself jobless during the Depression. In Tokyo for a big opportunity that falls apart, he meets a Japanese agent and his Russian colleague, and the pilot suddenly finds himself caught in a web of intrigue. Peter Lorre played Mr. Moto in a series of popular films. **Introduction by Lawrence Block.**

**Nancy Barr Mavity, *The Tule Marsh Murder*.** In this mystery inspired by a real case that captivated the San Francisco Bay Area in the 1920s, newspaper reporter Peter Piper teams up with psychologist Dr. Cavanaugh to investigate a woman's body found burnt beyond recognition. The cutting-edge forensics in the story were based on the pioneering work of criminalist Edward Oscar Heinrich who became known as "America's Sherlock Holmes." **Introduction by Randall Brandt.**

**Stuart Palmer, *The Penguin Pool Murder*.** The first adventure of schoolteacher and dedicated amateur sleuth Hildegarde Withers occurs at the New York Aquarium when she and her young students notice a corpse in one of the tanks. It was published in 1931 and filmed the next year, starring Edna May Oliver as the American Miss Marple—though much funnier than her English counterpart. **Introduction by Otto Penzler.**

**Stuart Palmer, *The Puzzle of the Happy Hooligan*.** New York City schoolteacher Hildegarde Withers cannot resist "assisting" homicide detective Oliver Piper. In this novel, she is on vacation in Hollywood and on the set of a movie about Lizzie Borden when the screenwriter is found dead. Six comic films about Withers appeared in the 1930s, most successfully starring Edna May Oliver. **Introduction by Otto Penzler.**

**Q. Patrick, *S.S. Murder*.** Cub reporter Mary Llewellyn's pleasant sea cruise sours when a wealthy businessman dies from drinking strychnine in his cocktail, and another passenger is shoved overboard in a connected murder. Mary takes it upon herself to snoop above and below deck to get to the truth and halt this seafaring slayer's onslaught. **Introduction by Curtis Evans.**

**Otto Penzler, ed., *Golden Age Bibliomysteries*.** Stories of murder, theft, and suspense occur with alarming regularity in the unlikely world of books and bibliophiles, including bookshops, libraries, and private rare book collections, written by such giants of the mystery genre as Ellery Queen, Cornell Woolrich, Lawrence G. Blochman, Vincent Starrett, and Anthony Boucher. **Introduction by Otto Penzler.**

**Otto Penzler, ed., *Golden Age Christmas Mysteries*.** Christmas has served as a fertile background for mystery fiction for a very long time and many of the stories in this anthology are undoubtedly inspired by the juxtaposition of the disparate elements of love and hate, written by such giants of the genre as Ellery

Queen, Mary Roberts Rinehart, John D. MacDonald, and John Dickson Carr. **Introduction by Otto Penzler.**

**Otto Penzler, ed.,** ***Golden Age Detective Stories.*** The history of American mystery fiction has its pantheon of authors who have influenced and entertained readers for nearly a century, reaching its peak during the Golden Age, and this collection pays homage to the work of the most acclaimed: Cornell Woolrich, Erle Stanley Gardner, Craig Rice, Ellery Queen, Dorothy B. Hughes, Mary Roberts Rinehart, and more. **Introduction by Otto Penzler.**

**Otto Penzler, ed.,** ***Golden Age Locked Room Mysteries.*** The so-called impossible crime category reached its zenith during the 1920s, 1930s, and 1940s, and this volume includes the greatest of the great authors who mastered the form: John Dickson Carr, Ellery Queen, C. Daly King, Clayton Rawson, and Erle Stanley Gardner. Like great magicians, these literary conjurors will baffle and delight readers. **Introduction by Otto Penzler.**

**Otto Penzler, ed.,** ***Golden Age Suspense Stories.*** Rarely classified as whodunits, suspense stories are more accurately described as "when-will-it-be-dones." From hungry tigers stalking their prey to jealous lovers plotting revenge, the binding element is anticipation. This collection selects the highlights of the genre with familiar names such as Stanley Ellin, James M. Cain, and Ellery Queen, alongside lesser known authors worth revisiting. **Introduction by Otto Penzler.**

**Otto Penzler, ed.,** ***Golden Age Whodunits.*** This collection of fifteen puzzling tales is a cross-section from an era when the whodunit flourished. These short mysteries were published far and wide by a variety of authors, such as the masters of the genre featured in this volume: F. Scott Fitzgerald, Ellery Queen, Mary Roberts Rinehart, Ring Lardner, Melville Davisson Post, Helen Reilly, and more. **Introduction by Otto Penzler.**

**Ellery Queen,** ***The Adventures of Ellery Queen.*** These stories are the earliest short works to feature Queen as a detective and are among the best of the author's fair-play mysteries. So many of the elements that comprise the gestalt of Queen may be found in these tales: alternate solutions, the dying clue, a bizarre crime, and the author's ability to find fresh variations of works by other authors. **Introduction by Otto Penzler.**

**Ellery Queen,** ***The American Gun Mystery.*** A rodeo comes to New York City at the Colosseum. The headliner is Buck Horne, the once popular film cowboy who opens the show leading a charge of forty whooping cowboys until they pull out their guns and fire into the air. Buck falls to the ground, shot dead. The police instantly lock the doors to search everyone but the offending weapon has completely vanished. **Introduction by Otto Penzler.**

**Ellery Queen,** ***Cat of Many Tails.*** In the summertime, a serial killer called the Cat preys on New Yorkers seemingly at random, strangles them, and miraculously escapes without a trace. It is now the 1940s, and Ellery Queen, the brilliant amateur sleuth, is retired, but he pounces on a chance to crack the case when he discovers a clue that could hold the secret to untangling the puzzling crimes. **Introduction by Richard Dannay.**

**Ellery Queen,** ***The Chinese Orange Mystery.*** The offices of publisher Donald Kirk have seen strange events but nothing like this. A strange man is found dead with two long spears alongside his back. And, though no one was seen entering or leaving the room, everything has been turned backwards or upside down: pictures face the wall, the victim's clothes are worn backwards, the rug upside down. Why in the world? **Introduction by Otto Penzler.**

**Ellery Queen,** ***The Dutch Shoe Mystery.*** Millionaire philanthropist Abagail Doorn falls into a coma and she is rushed to the hospital she funds for an emergency operation by one of the leading surgeons on the East Coast. When she is wheeled into the operating theater, the sheet covering her body is pulled back to reveal her garroted corpse—the first of a series of murders. **Introduction by Otto Penzler.**

**Ellery Queen,** ***The Egyptian Cross Mystery.*** A small-town schoolteacher is found dead, beheaded, and tied to a T-shaped cross on December 25th, inspiring such sensational headlines as "Crucifixion on Christmas Day." Amateur sleuth Ellery Queen is so intrigued he travels to Virginia but fails to solve the crime. Then a similar murder takes place on New York's Long Island—and then another. **Introduction by Otto Penzler.**

**Ellery Queen,** ***The Siamese Twin Mystery.*** When Ellery and his father encounter a raging forest fire on a mountain, their only hope is to drive up to an isolated hillside manor owned by a secretive surgeon and his strange guests. While playing solitaire in the middle of the night, the doctor is shot. The only clue is a torn playing card. Suspects include a society beauty, a valet, and conjoined twins. **Introduction by Otto Penzler.**

**Ellery Queen, *The Spanish Cape Mystery.*** Amateur detective Ellery Queen arrives in the resort town of Spanish Cape soon after a young woman and her uncle are abducted by a gun-toting, one-eyed giant. The next day, the woman's somewhat dicey boyfriend is found murdered—totally naked under a black fedora and opera cloak. **Introduction by Otto Penzler.**

**Ellery Queen, *The Tragedy of X.*** Using his powers of disguise, knowledge of human nature, and an occasional dash of theatrical combat, the majestic old-fashioned thespian Drury Lane is the most fantastic detective of all time—onstage or off. After a man is poisoned on a crowded New York streetcar, not one of the witnesses can provide any evidence. The police are stumped until they receive a letter from Lane, claiming to have solved the crime. **Introduction by Otto Penzler.**

**Ellery Queen, *The Tragedy of Y.*** A ramshackle trawler rumbling through New York harbor spots something floating in the water. Dragging it in, they find the limp, cold, and bloody corpse of York Hatter, who had disappeared several days before. Solving the case will fall to Drury Lane, the retired Shakespearean actor turned his crime-solving genius. But he may find that these Hatters are so mad and so deadly. **Introduction by Otto Penzler.**

**Patrick Quentin, *A Puzzle for Fools.*** Broadway producer Peter Duluth takes to the bottle when his wife dies but enters a sanitarium to dry out. Malevolent events plague the hospital, including when Peter hears his own voice intone, "There will be murder." And there is. He investigates, aided by a young woman who is also a patient. This is the first of nine mysteries featuring Peter and Iris Duluth. **Introduction by Otto Penzler.**

**Clayton Rawson, *Death from a Top Hat.*** When the New York City Police Department is baffled by an apparently impossible crime, they call on The Great Merlini, a retired stage magician who now runs a Times Square magic shop. In his first case, two occultists have been murdered in a room locked from the inside, their bodies positioned to form a pentagram. **Introduction by Otto Penzler.**

**Helen Reilly, *McKee of Centre Street.*** In one of the first-ever police procedurals written by a woman, a famous dancer is murdered in a New York speakeasy. Everyone in the crowd is an eligible suspect for Inspector McKee of the NYPD, who examines the witness statements and pieces together a rich and confounding story of blackmail and stolen emeralds. **Introduction by Otto Penzler.**

**Craig Rice, *Eight Faces at Three.*** Gin-soaked John J. Malone, defender of the guilty, is notorious for getting his culpable clients off. It's the innocent ones who are problems. Like Holly Inglehart, accused of piercing the black heart of her well-heeled Aunt Alexandria with a lovely Florentine paper cutter. No one who knew the old battle-ax liked her, but Holly's prints were found on the murder weapon. **Introduction by Lisa Lutz.**

**Craig Rice, *Home Sweet Homicide.*** Known as the Dorothy Parker of mystery fiction for her memorable wit, Craig Rice was the first detective writer to appear on the cover of *Time* magazine. This comic mystery features two kids who are trying to find a husband for their widowed mother while she's engaged in sleuthing. Filmed with the same title in 1946 with Peggy Ann Garner and Randolph Scott. **Introduction by Otto Penzler.**

**Mary Roberts Rinehart, *The Album.*** Crescent Place is a quiet enclave of wealthy people in which nothing ever happens—until a bedridden old woman is attacked by an intruder with an ax. *The New York Times* stated: "All Mary Roberts Rinehart mystery stories are good, but this one is better." **Introduction by Otto Penzler.**

**Mary Roberts Rinehart, *The Door.*** Elizabeth Bell runs a quiet household but the old woman's life is upended when a young cousin comes to visit and the nurse vanishes while taking the dogs for a walk. Then the nurse is found murdered and police insist that the killer must be one of the household. More deaths are quick to follow in this atmospheric whodunit bursting with family secrets and period details. **Introduction by Otto Penzler.**

**Mary Roberts Rinehart, *The Great Mistake.*** Maud Wainwright rules in her elaborate house known as the Cloisters, but recent attacks on her estate and a shocking murder threaten her power. Thankfully, her right-hand woman, Pat Abbott, is determined to unmask Maud's enemy hiding among her crowd of high-society friends. Pat also endeavors to protect Maud's married son, whom she secretly adores. **Introduction by Otto Penzler.**

**Mary Roberts Rinehart, *The Haunted Lady.*** The arsenic in her sugar bowl was wealthy widow Eliza Fairbanks' first clue that somebody wanted her dead. Nightly visits of bats, birds, and rats, obviously aimed at scaring the dowager to death, was the second. Eliza calls the police, who send nurse Hilda Adams, the amateur sleuth they refer to as "Miss Pinkerton," to work undercover to discover the culprit. **Introduction by Otto Penzler.**

**Mary Roberts Rinehart, *Miss Pinkerton.*** Hilda Adams is a nurse, not a detective, but she is observant and smart and so it is common for Inspector Patton to call on her for help. Her success results in his calling her "Miss Pinkerton." *The New Republic* wrote: "From thousands of hearts and homes the cry will go up: Thank God for Mary Roberts Rinehart." **Introduction by Carolyn Hart.**

**Mary Roberts Rinehart, *The Red Lamp.*** Professor William Porter refuses to believe that the seaside manor he's just inherited is haunted, but he has to convince his wife to move in. However, he soon sees evidence of the occult phenomena of which the townspeople speak. Whether it is a spirit or a human being, Porter accepts that there is a connection to the rash of murders that have terrorized the countryside. **Introduction by Otto Penzler.**

**Mary Roberts Rinehart, *The Wall.*** For two decades, Mary Roberts Rinehart was the second-best-selling author in America (only Sinclair Lewis outsold her) and was beloved for her tales of suspense. In one of her most popular cozy mysteries, set in a magnificent mansion, the ex-wife of one of the owners turns up making demands and is found dead the next day. And there are more dark secrets lying behind the walls of the estate. **Introduction by Otto Penzler.**

**Mary Roberts Rinehart, *The Yellow Room.*** When her husband is shot down over the South Pacific, Carol finds herself on the verge of spinsterhood at twenty-four. Her invalid mother demands that she accompany her to the family's summer home in Maine. But there is a killer on the grounds of the abandoned estate, and the police believe it is Carol. As war rages across the seas, Carol fights to prove her own innocence and to save her mother's life. **Introduction by Otto Penzler.**

**Rutledge, Nancy, *Blood on the Cat.*** Bennet Farr was the richest, most corrupt, and most hated man in Cognac, a small Chicago suburb. So when he is found dead one morning, the chief of police faces a long line of suspects. Reporter Killian McBean is among them. His journalistic acumen cuts through the noise in search of the real story—though it's his cat Smoky that discovers the essential clue that leads to its solution. **Introduction by Otto Penzler.**

**Hake Talbot, *Rim of the Pit.*** A family conducts a seance at a snow-bound lodge to ask their dead father if they can sell his treasured pine grove, and then one of them ends up dead in a locked room. This impossible murder with an inexplicable trail of footprints and a gun hung high out of reach defies logic and suggests a supernatural presence in this creepy Golden Age cult classic. **Introduction by Rupert Holmes.**

**Joel Townsley Rogers, *The Red Right Hand.*** This extraordinary whodunit is as puzzling as it is terrifying. Identified by crime fiction scholar Jack Adrian as "one of the dozen or so finest mystery novels of the 20th century." A deranged killer sends a doctor on a quest for the truth—deep into the recesses of his own mind—when he and his bride-to-be elope but pick up a terrifying sharp-toothed hitchhiker. **Introduction by Joe R. Lansdale.**

**Roger Scarlett, *Cat's Paw.*** The family of the wealthy old bachelor Martin Greenough cares far more about his money than they do about him. For his birthday, he invites all his potential heirs to his mansion to tell them what they hope to hear. Before he can disburse funds, however, he is murdered, and the Boston Police Department's big problem is that there are too many suspects. **Introduction by Curtis Evans.**

**Jonathan Stagge, *The Scarlet Circle.*** On vacation with his daughter on the New England coast, Dr. Hugh Westlake is enjoying the sun and the sea, and fishing. It being September, the inn where they're staying is almost empty, except for a few other guests. But the peace is shattered when a woman's body is found strangled on the beach with a red circle drawn around a mole on her face. **Introduction by Otto Penzler.**

**Vincent Starrett, *Dead Man Inside.*** 1930s Chicago is a tough town but some crimes are more bizarre than others. Customers arrive at a haberdasher to find a corpse in the window and a sign on the door: *Dead Man Inside! I am Dead. The store will not open today*. This is just one of a series of odd murders that terrorizes the city. Reluctant detective Walter Ghost leaps into action to learn what is behind the plague. **Introduction by Otto Penzler.**

**Vincent Starrett, *The Great Hotel Murder*.** Theater critic and amateur sleuth Riley Blackwood investigates a murder in a Chicago hotel where the dead man had changed rooms with a stranger who had registered under a fake name. *The New York Times* described it as "an ingenious plot with enough complications to keep the reader guessing." **Introduction by Lyndsay Faye.**

**Vincent Starrett, *Murder on "B" Deck*.** Walter Ghost, a psychologist, scientist, explorer, and former intelligence officer, is on a cruise ship. His friend, novelist Dunsten Mollock, a Nigel Bruce-like Watson whose role is to offer occasional comic relief, accommodates when he fails to leave the ship before it takes off. Although they make mistakes along the way, the amateur sleuths solve the shipboard murders. **Introduction by Ray Betzner.**

**Phoebe Atwood Taylor, *The Cape Cod Mystery*.** Vacationers have flocked to Cape Cod to avoid the heat wave that hit the Northeast and find their holiday unpleasant when the area is flooded with police trying to find the murderer of a muckraking journalist who took a cottage for the season. Finding a solution falls to Asey Mayo, "the Cape Cod Sherlock," known for his worldly wisdom, folksy humor, and common sense. **Introduction by Otto Penzler.**

**Phoebe Atwood Taylor, *The Mystery of the Cape Cod Tavern*.** In a small Cape Cod town, a local tavern owner is convinced that someone is trying to kill her. Others in the village think she's just out for free publicity. Until she's found stabbed to death. Man-about-town and jack-of-all-trades Asey Mayo is helping out at the tavern when the murder occurs, and he's just the sleuth that such a dastardly case needs. But will he succeed before an innocent person takes the fall? **Introduction by Otto Penzler.**

**Phoebe Atwood Taylor, *Sandbar Sinister*.** After a bootlegger dumps two hundred cases of liquor off the beaches of Cape Cod, the whole town of East Pochet endeavors to drink it before the hooch can be impounded. When the fog of revelry lifts, however, a bearded mystery writer and one other are found dead on the Sandbar estate. As every clue reveals a new question, Asey Mayo finds himself investigating one of the trickiest cases of his career. **Introduction by Otto Penzler.**

**S. S. Van Dine, *The Benson Murder Case*.** The first of 12 novels to feature Philo Vance, the most popular and influential detective character of the early part of the 20th century. When wealthy stockbroker Alvin Benson is found shot to death in a locked room in his mansion, the police are baffled until the erudite flaneur and art collector arrives on the scene. Paramount filmed it in 1930 with William Powell as Vance. **Introduction by Ragnar Jónasson.**

**S.S. Van Dine, *The Greene Murder Case*.** The heirs in the illustrious Greene family die one after the other as an elusive killer stalks their New York City mansion and fires shots at them. Part-time supersleuth Philo Vance consults detailed floor plans, fairly clued testimonies, and the obscure texts in the family's secret criminology library to provide his brilliant solution to this third mystery in his detective saga. **Introduction by Otto Penzler.**

**Cornell Woolrich, *The Bride Wore Black*.** The first suspense novel by one of the greatest of all noir authors opens with a bride and her new husband walking out of the church. A car speeds by, shots ring out, and he falls dead at her feet. Determined to avenge his death, she tracks down everyone in the car, concluding with a shocking surprise. It was filmed by Francois Truffaut in 1968, starring Jeanne Moreau. **Introduction by Eddie Muller.**

**Cornell Woolrich, *Deadline at Dawn*.** Quinn is overcome with guilt about having robbed a stranger's home. He meets Bricky, a dime-a-dance girl, and they fall for each other. When they return to the crime scene, they discover a dead body. Knowing Quinn will be accused of the crime, they race to find the true killer before he's arrested. A 1946 film starring Susan Hayward was loosely based on the plot. **Introduction by David Gordon.**

**Cornell Woolrich, *Waltz into Darkness*.** A New Orleans businessman successfully courts a woman through the mail but he is shocked to find when she arrives that she is not the plain brunette whose picture he'd received but a radiant blond beauty. She soon absconds with his fortune. Wracked with disappointment and loneliness, he vows to track her down. When he finds her, the real nightmare begins. **Introduction by Wallace Stroby.**

**Lassiter Wren & Randle McKay, *The Baffle Book*.** Calling all mystery puzzle fans! This book launched the "solve-it-yourself" detective book craze of the 1920s and '30s. These thirty short crime problems incorporate all of the clues needed to find their solutions, including maps, charts, cryptograms, and additional illustrations—but it's up to the reader to put all of this together and find out whodunit. **Introduction by Otto Penzler.**